JACK JONES

AND THE

PIRATE CURSE

JACK JONES
AND THE
PIRATE CURSE

JUDITH ROSSELL

WALKER & COMPANY
NEW YORK

Published in the United States of America in 2007 by
Walker Publishing Company, Inc.
Distributed to the trade by Holtzbrinck Publishers

First published in Australia in 2006 by Little Hare Books

For information about permission to reproduce selections from
this book, write to Permissions, Walker & Company,
104 Fifth Avenue, New York, New York 10011

Library of Congress Cataloging-in-Publication Data
Rossell, Judith.
Jack Jones and the pirate curse / Judith Rossell.
p.   cm.
First published in 2006 by Little Hare Books.
Summary: With the death of his Great-Uncle Mungo, Jack learns to his dismay
that, as the tenth-generation descendant of the Caribbean pirate Blackstrap
Morgan, he is next in line to inherit the Pirate Curse and is fated to spend his life
running from a vengeful band of pirates—unless he finds a way to outsmart them.
ISBN-13: 978-0-8027-9661-5 • ISBN-10: 0-8027-9661-3 (hardcover)
[1. Pirates—Fiction. 2. Blessing and cursing—Fiction. 3. Parrots—Fiction.
4. Adventure and adventurers—Fiction.] I. Title.
PZ7.R719983Jac 2007   [Fic]—dc22   2006052554

Visit Walker & Company's Web site at www.walkeryoungreaders.com

Typeset in Stone Serif by Asset Typesetting Pty Ltd
Printed in the U.S.A. by Quebecor World Fairfield
2 4 6 8 10 9 7 5 3 1

All papers used by Walker & Company are natural, recyclable products
made from wood grown in well-managed forests. The manufacturing processes
conform to the environmental regulations of the country of origin.

For Ali Lavau, editor and pirate queen

CHAPTER 1

The first strange thing happened after school. Until then it had been like every other Wednesday.

Jack was waiting outside the classroom for his friend and next-door neighbor, Rachel. She was being told off by Mrs. Lemon for wearing pink ribbons—which were not part of the school uniform—and for arguing about it.

Mothers were standing in groups, chatting. Little kids were running around.

Suddenly, Jack felt a shudder run through him. It was the strangest feeling. He felt it through his feet and in the air around him. It was as if someone had just slammed a very heavy door nearby. Or maybe dropped an enormous rock onto the ground. But there was no sound, only the feeling. And then it was gone.

He looked around, startled. For a moment, everything looked different. Somehow brighter and clearer, more sharply focused. He had the odd sensation that something important had happened. But what?

Nobody else seemed to have noticed anything. People were still talking, laughing. Kids were still running around. Jack shook his head, a bit dizzy.

Rachel shot out of the classroom, looked around for a moment, and spotted Jack. "Come on, come on," she said, as if he had been keeping her waiting. "Let's get going. Crazy old cow. Anyone would think I was some kind of mass murderer or one of those people on *America's Most Wanted*. Pink ribbons! I mean, they're not illegal."

"Did you get a really weird feeling just then?" asked Jack.

"What kind of feeling?" asked Rachel. "I had the feeling I was going to say, 'Mrs. Lemon, you can just—'"

"No, no," interrupted Jack. "Like—I don't know—like a big thud? Like an earthquake or something?"

Rachel looked at him strangely. "No."

Jack shrugged. "Well, I felt something."

On Wednesdays, Jack had pocket money for an after-school snack. Rachel walked with him to the Food Quick store on the corner. Jack always bought a green soda and a bag of Cheetos. Sometimes Rachel got something and sometimes not. Today, she chose a pink donut with colored sprinkles.

As they went to pay, Rachel continued with her complaints about Mrs. Lemon. "I should spray my hair pink, you know. Or paint my whole head. She wouldn't like that. Oh no. She wouldn't like that at all. There's no school rule about painting your head."

"Well, you'd know," said Jack. Mrs. Lemon's usual punishment for wearing things that were not part of the school uniform was to make the offender copy out the school uniform rules. Rachel had copied them out many, many times. This had made her a school uniform rule expert.

Jack plunked the bottle of green soda and the bag of Cheetos up on the counter and fished his wallet out of his pocket. The teenager behind the counter picked up the things to scan them. His name tag said HELLO, MY NAME IS STEWART, which was more than Stewart himself ever said. He only ever said prices and grunted.

Expecting he would say, "Two fifty," just like he always did, Jack unzipped his wallet to get the money out.

But then a second strange thing happened.

Stewart stood up, leaned over the counter toward Jack, and yelled in a very loud, hoarse voice, "Har har har, Blackstrap's brat. You little bilge rat. We'll be seeing you in Davy Jones's locker, by thunder. Har har har."

Jack jumped backward like a startled kangaroo, bumping into Rachel. Stewart's face had twisted into a mean leer. It was almost unrecognizable. Jack saw a shiny gold tooth in his mouth, and a gold earring in one ear. Had they been there before? The new, frightening Stewart leaned toward them, waving the bottle of green soda threateningly.

"Blackstrap's brat," he shouted. "We'll be seeing the color of your insides, by the powers. Har har har."

"What?" gasped Jack, edging past, getting ready to run for the exit.

"Two fifty, I said," grunted Stewart, suddenly back to normal, slouching and staring off into space. No earring. No gold tooth.

"No, no thanks." Jack backed toward the door, trying to keep as far out of reach as he could, leaving the green soda and the bag of Cheetos on the counter.

Rachel followed, scuttling past the counter, stumbling over her own feet in her haste. As she passed Stewart, she nervously flung the pink donut at him. "Sorry," she said. "Changed my mind . . . Got to go now."

They dashed to the exit and jumped up and down, flapping their arms, to open the automatic doors.

"Hurry!" Jack looked back and saw Stewart watching them with an expression of mild surprise. Then they were outside. They sprinted through the parking lot, along the footpath, and across the road, and they didn't stop running until they reached the corner of their own street.

Jack leaned against a telephone pole, panting painfully. "What was that all about?"

Rachel shrugged, out of breath. "Maybe it was a student thing. A joke," she gasped.

"Weird, though," said Jack. "Did you see that earring?"

"What? No. What earring?"

"In his ear. I think I saw it, anyway," said Jack. He shivered. "Scary."

Rachel nodded. "It was like he changed into someone else, but only for a few seconds. I've never seen anything like it before. Maybe he's an actor, and he's rehearsing a part. Or maybe it's National Talk-Like-a-Frightening-Pirate-Unexpectedly Day."

"Maybe," said Jack. *But that wasn't acting,* he thought to himself. *That was real.*

Jack decided to tell his mom and dad about it during dinner. No doubt, there was a sensible explanation for the strange and scary thing that had happened, and then they would all laugh about it, and Jack would feel much better.

They always ate at the table, never in front of the TV like some families. They were eating pasta with red sauce and mushrooms. Jack's parents had red wine to drink and Jack had green soda, which his father thought was bad for his teeth. They talked a bit about school and work. Jack's father told stories about how he had put fillings in the teeth of people who drank such things as green soda.

Jack thought this might be a good time to change the subject, so he told his parents what had happened that afternoon at Food Quick. When he finished the story, he waited for the laughter and the sensible explanation.

Instead, there was a long silence. Jack started to feel worse, not better, especially when he saw a look pass between his mom and dad. It was one of those looks that means secrets and adult mysteries.

"But the crazy old buzzard's still alive, isn't he?" asked Dad.

What? thought Jack. *What buzzard?*

Mom looked down at her plate and, after a moment, said, "As far as I know . . ."

Dad looked a bit annoyed and Mom looked a bit nervous and uncertain. Jack looked from one to the other. "What's going on?" he asked, feeling a bit like he was standing on the edge of a cliff. "Who's still alive? What are you talking about?"

Mom cleared her throat. "It's your great-uncle Mungo we're talking about, darling. It's possible he's . . . Well, it seems like . . ." Her voice trailed off. Then she said more firmly, "I'll just make a call. I won't be a minute."

She went out, closing the door carefully behind her. Jack looked across at his dad, who was frowning and scooping pasta into his mouth automatically. "What's going on?" he asked.

Dad grimaced, shook his head, and kept on eating.

Mom came back and sat down.

"Well?" asked Dad.

Mom nodded, looking worried.

Jack said, "What? What's going on?"

"I'm sorry, darling," said Mom. "It's Great-Uncle Mungo. He died today."

"Oh," said Jack blankly. "That's . . . that's sad."

"Yes," said Mom. "I'm sorry. He was your godfather as well, remember."

"I never met him, though," said Jack.

"Well, India's a long way away. He was at your christening."

Jack really was sorry to hear about Great-Uncle Mungo. Although Jack had been only a tiny baby the last time they had met, and of course he couldn't remember that, he had often wanted to see him again. For one thing,

Great-Uncle Mungo had always sent the strangest presents. And not for Jack's birthday or for Christmas, but at odd times. There had been a really beautiful gold cigarette lighter, for example, with red stones on the sides, which Jack's father thought might be real rubies. An unusual present for a ten-year-old. Then a pair of what might have been belt buckles, but with curly gold edges and lots of glittery jewels set in them. And after that the little knife, which was probably the least appropriate present of all, because its blade was so sharp it could cut holes in the dining table. It had taken Jack a fair amount of persuading before his parents allowed him to keep that.

As well, there was a small hoard of coins from all over the world. There were tiny ones as small as sequins, some with holes in them like little metal donuts, square ones, and ones with palm trees on them. Jack had made a wooden box at school and he kept all of Great-Uncle Mungo's presents in it. He looked at them often. They were the best things he had.

Jack took a calming sip of green soda and said, "But Mom, how did you know to call?

What's Great-Uncle Mungo got to do with Stewart at Food Quick today? Something weird is going on, isn't it?"

Mom opened her mouth to answer, but before any words came out they were startled by a loud bang, like a door slamming shut in the wind, and a flurry of green feathers as a parrot appeared on the dining table.

There was a stunned silence.

Jack's father paused with his fork halfway into his mouth and just sat there, with his mouth hanging open. Mom was so surprised her hand twitched and a forkful of pasta shot across the room and splattered on the wall. Jack choked on a mouthful of green soda and stared in amazement at the brilliant green parrot who was perched on the edge of the bowl of pasta and sauce.

The parrot gave a cluck, a bit like a chicken, looked around the table with an intelligent expression, and settled its gaze on Jack.

"Jack Jones?" The bird cocked its head on one side and regarded him through beady black eyes.

"Yes," said Jack, who was too surprised to say anything else.

"Poll," said the parrot, extending one foot. Cautiously, Jack put out a finger, and they shook—not hands, obviously, but finger and foot.

"Jack, Jack," said the parrot, hopping down onto the table, leaving several red footprints on the white tablecloth. "Named, I presume, for the great Calico Jack, terror of the Caribbean."

"What? No," said Jack.

"Jack Plantain, pirate king of Madagascar?"

"I don't think so."

"Not Jack Hawkins, the black-hearted slave trader?"

"No!"

"Well, that's something, shipmate." Poll skipped a couple of steps down the table and noticed for the first time the stunned faces of Jack's parents. "But Jack, your crew seems to be caught adrift . . . Surely you were expecting me?"

"Er, not really," admitted Jack.

"But now that Mungo Morgan has gone to Davy Jones—well, sink me . . . D'ye not know who I am?"

Jack could only shake his head.

"Well, then." Poll paused dramatically, gave a

low bow, just missing the margarine with his beak, and announced, "Jack, shipmate, you be the tenth direct descendant of Blackstrap Morgan, Terror of the South Seas, Traitor to the Brethren of the Coast. And I . . ."—he paused and looked around the table—"I am the Pirate Curse." He paused again, then added, less impressively, "Well, part of it, anyway."

 # CHAPTER 2

Jack's mom came suddenly back to life. "Oh no," she said, holding her head in her hands. "So it's really happening. I never thought . . . I mean . . . oh no."

Dad interrupted, "Your family! That crazy uncle and now this. I knew it. Pirates, for heaven's sake." He looked at the sauce-splattered table, which was normally so lovely, clean, and white. Dad liked things to be clean. "I can't believe this nonsense," he said angrily, standing up. "No. Not in this house."

"But won't you—," began Mom.

"No," said Dad. "And anyway, what could I do? I don't know the first thing about pirates. I'm going to do laps in the pool." He marched to the door. "But I'd like to see that . . . that"—he jabbed a finger at Poll—"that *thing* gone when I get back." As he left the room he snapped, "And for your information, bird, Jack was named for Sir Jack Fangbright, Legendary Dentist and Terror to Tartar. Ha!" He slammed the door. Jack jumped.

Mom jumped too. She picked up a piece of bread and tried to mop up some of the drops of sauce with it. Her hands were jerking in a nervous kind of way.

Jack started to feel sick. He'd never seen his mom so anxious. His dad never slammed doors. Strange parrots never appeared in the dining room and started talking about pirates.

Mom cleared her throat, and then said in a rush, "I'm sorry, Jack. I know I should have warned you about this. But the truth is, I never really believed in the curse. Still, I suppose with Uncle Mungo being like he was, I should have realized . . . I guess I just hoped it would never happen."

"What?" asked Jack. "Hoped what wouldn't happen? What curse? What's going on?"

Mom was crumbling the bread between her fingers. It didn't look like she was going to answer him.

"Mom?" he said urgently.

Reluctantly, she looked up. "Well, Jack, it's like this." She sighed. "Our family is cursed. It's a pirate curse. I know it sounds ridiculous. I mean, it sounds so . . ." She waved a shaking hand from side to side. "You know. Anyway, it's meant to pass down through the family. And with Uncle Mungo dead, you're the next in line, and it seems like you've inherited it. What happened in Food Quick today was the start of it. And now the parrot's arrived."

They both looked at Poll, who had settled down to clean the sauce off his feathers, one by one. He looked up and gave a polite cluck.

"But what does it mean?" said Jack. "What's going to happen?"

Mom said, "I've never really known about it. Uncle Mungo was always traveling, so I never saw much of him. And he was such a strange man, what with that eye patch—and, of course, the parrot. He always seemed to be looking over his shoulder. Very jumpy. At your christening, he got into a fight with an enormous man with a big red beard, who suddenly appeared in the street outside the church. It was very peculiar; one second Uncle Mungo was standing next to this sweet old lady, and the next second there was this hairy giant . . ." Mom's voice trailed off again.

Jack looked at her for a moment, feeling

completely confused. He turned to the parrot. "What's this all about?"

"Well, shipmate," said Poll, "it's a long story. Particularly the way I tell it. A story of Love and Betrayal. Well, not Love, in truth—mainly Betrayal. Betrayal and Revenge. Your ancestor, Blackstrap Morgan, sent his comrades to the gallows at Port Royal. With their dying breaths they cursed him. A terrible Curse, shipmate, a Curse to freeze the blood in your veins, just to hear it. And the Curse was for his sons and his sons' sons and down through the generations. A mighty powerful Curse, shipmate."

"Yes, okay," said Jack. "But that all happened years ago. Years and years and years. What about now? What's going to happen to me?"

"Shipmate," said Poll, "the crew were powerful angry with Blackstrap, and now they're powerful angry with you. It's all about Revenge. They want their Revenge, by the powers."

Jack thought about that for a moment. "So you're saying they want a fight?"

"Indeed, shipmate. They want a fight."

"And like in Food Quick this afternoon, and

like at my christening with Uncle Mungo, people can turn into pirates? Is that it? Anyone can turn into a pirate and start a fight with me?"

"That's the truth of it, shipmate," said Poll cheerfully.

Mom gave a moan and clutched her head with her hands. Jack felt like doing the same thing. "No, no," he said. "No way." He tried to think. At last he asked, "How can I stop it?"

"It's not possible, shipmate," said Poll. "The Curse will last your lifetime, and then be passed on down the family. It's lasted ten generations so far, and it's not getting any weaker, by thunder."

Jack couldn't get a grip on this. No wonder Mom hadn't really believed in the family curse. It was unbelievable. But it was happening to him. What could he do? He shook his head, attempting to clear his thoughts. He opened his mouth to say something, shut it again, opened it again, and finally said, "Then what can I do about it?"

"Fight, shipmate," said Poll enthusiastically. "Ha ha ha. You've some prodigious battles on your horizon, by thunder. The scuppers will run with blood, to be sure."

Hearing this, Mom laid her hands flat on the tabletop. Jack was relieved to see she had stopped fiddling with the bread and was starting to look a bit more like herself. Mom could sort out anything. She would sort out these pirates.

She took a deep, calm breath. "Right," she said. "First of all, Jack, stop worrying. I'm sure we can deal with this. It's just a matter of approaching it in the right way."

Jack immediately felt more hopeful. When Mom dealt with things, they got fixed. That's how it worked. She had looked overwhelmed for a short while, but now she was back to normal. Soon everything would be fine.

"Second," Mom went on, "don't leave the house. Why don't you go upstairs and do your homework or your keyboard practice or something like that? I'll go and make some phone calls. That's the best idea. Get some information."

Jack nodded.

Mom stood up and gave him a quick hug. "It seems to me that a family curse must be genetic. Like dyslexia, or red hair, or other things that run in families. I'll call that genetics professor at the university. She'll know what to do. Or that pediatrician I met at the school committee meeting last month. I'm sure he sees things like this all the time. And there's always the Internet. Don't worry, Jack, I'll get to the bottom of this. Leave it to me." She smiled. "Okay?"

"Okay," agreed Jack. He gave a relieved sigh as Mom marched off with a determined look on her face, and he turned to Poll, who was still preening himself.

"Shipmate," said the parrot, "I've a powerful hunger on me. Any chance of a noggin of something?"

Jack didn't know what Poll might like to eat, so he took him into the kitchen to see what they had. Poll perched on Jack's head, his bright beady eyes scanning the contents of the fridge, his claws gripping painfully onto Jack's scalp.

"A tot of grog would go down a treat, shipmate," he said encouragingly.

"Grog?"

"Grog," repeated Poll. "Rotgut. Black Ruin."

"What?"

"Rum, shipmate."

"Well," said Jack doubtfully, "I'm not sure we've got any. How about green soda?"

Poll sampled the green soda thoughtfully. "Not bad, shipmate—at any rate, an excellent color." He drank some more, burped loudly, and remarked, "A lively drop, puts wind up my vittles." Poll finished the drink, gave a few more burps, and looked expectantly into the fridge. "A bit of ship's biscuit, or plum duff, mayhap?"

Jack offered him various things from the fridge. Poll bit a carrot in half, but let the pieces fall onto the floor. He dipped his beak experimentally into some yogurt, spat violently, and asked Jack if this was really food, or if it was in fact a poisoning attempt. Despite the nervous feeling lurking in his stomach, Jack giggled.

He found a piece of his dad's special cheese, which Poll liked, and an orange, which the parrot took in one foot and ripped apart enthusiastically, spraying the kitchen with juice and bits of peel. In the pantry, Jack found several more things, including a bottle of

Tabasco sauce, which Poll enjoyed immensely. He confided that he had developed a taste for spicy food during his years in India with Great-Uncle Mungo. Finally, Jack emptied a box of muesli onto the kitchen counter, and Poll sorted through it to find the best parts—which were the nuts and seeds and the pieces of dried fruit—sweeping all the bran and oats onto the floor with his beak.

When they had finished, Jack looked around the kitchen. After eating all the food he wanted, Poll had done a jumping kind of dance called a hornpipe on the kitchen counter, and had managed to knock a lot of jars of herbs and spices onto the floor. They mixed with the yogurt and muesli and pieces of orange to make a sort of patchy food carpet. Jack had a feeling that his parents would not be at all happy about the mess.

Thinking about his parents made Jack wonder how his mom was getting on with finding things out about the curse. He hoped she would find the solution quickly. He didn't want to spend the rest of his life getting into fights with angry pirates.

He collected the broom and the dustpan and brush from the cupboard, and started to sweep up.

Poll watched him with interest. "That's right. Make everything shipshape," he remarked approvingly. Suddenly he burst into song. He had a surprisingly loud, rasping singing voice.

The Santa Infanta *sailed on the sea,*
From Santucky Head to Floridy Key,
She rocked and she rolled on the wind and
*   the tide,*
And everyone vomited over the side.

Poll sang with his eyes tight shut, hopping from foot to foot on the kitchen counter. The noise was terrible. The windowpanes were shaking, and the cups and saucers on the shelves were rattling. Jack poked his fingers into his ears, but even then he still felt his skull vibrating.

Poll sang the song several times through and finished with a piercing shriek. He fluffed himself up in a satisfied kind of way, and said, "Nothing like a shanty for getting the work done."

Jack couldn't help laughing. As if he could do anything much with his fingers stuffed in his ears. He supposed he should get on with his homework like his mom had suggested. "Come on," he said to Poll.

As they passed the study door, Jack could hear his mom talking on the phone. She sounded anxious. From the back window, he could see Dad doggedly swimming up and down the pool. Dad always swam laps when he was stressed. It didn't look like he was planning to stop anytime soon.

CHAPTER 3

"So this is your berth, shipmate." Poll looked around Jack's bedroom from his perch on the desk lamp. "Starboard cabin. Above the waterline. Rats?"

"Er, no," said Jack. "No rats."

"What's this?" Poll skipped across the desk and pounced on Jack's electronic keyboard. He jumped eagerly onto the keys, wings flapping, a few green feathers detaching themselves and drifting away. Nothing happened. Poll hopped up and down violently, and jabbed a few keys with his beak as well, but there was no result.

"It's not turned on," said Jack. He scooted his chair across the room and switched on the keyboard. Immediately, a mixed-up chord blurted out. Poll danced a few steps and produced a jumble of chords and random notes. He stabbed some of the buttons with his beak, making different sounds. He discovered the volume control and turned it up. Flapping his wings, he jumped hard onto the keys. The floor trembled and the windowpanes rattled. Jack was nearly deafened. Poll, however, was charmed.

"I do enjoy a rousing shanty, shipmate," he said, as the echoes faded away. "Blackstrap used to play in the Hanged Man in Tortuga. Mighty pretty it was, until he lost his hand. Can't play piano with a hook, shipmate. After that, he did the right hand and I did the left."

"What was—," Jack began, but at that moment, Poll started to play and sing. It was very, very loud. There was no chance for conversation. Jack couldn't even hear his own voice.

Poll played the keyboard by hopping from foot to foot, flapping his wings wildly for balance. He made some long leaps between notes, and he also did some impressive sliding runs. Jack couldn't help noticing that Poll's claws made little dents in the keys and his runs made skid marks.

The seas do howl and the winds do blow,
Down, down to Davy Jones they go,
All honest sailors sent below,
With a Yo ho ho and a Yo ho ho.

Jack didn't know the song. There was a chorus of Yo ho hos and verses about drowned pirates and Davy Jones's locker, and a gruesome part about coral growing out of a dead man's eyes. There was a lot about treasure, as well. The song seemed to have about twenty verses. Jack tried to interrupt a few times, but there was no way he could make himself heard.

There's treasure buried in the ground,
An island that cannot be found,
With sharks that circle all around,
Guarded by the pirates drowned.

Watching the strange parrot dancing around on the keyboard, Jack was starting to feel that things were getting out of hand. What had happened to his life? He glanced up above his desk, where schedules and lists were all stuck neatly in rows. The different activities were highlighted in different colors: green for chores, blue for homework, red for meals. Dad always said that a schedule put order into life. It kept things under control.

Today was Wednesday, for example. Wednesday's schedule read:

4:30 Home from school. Brush teeth
5:00 Television
5:30 Help prepare dinner. Discuss school day with parent. Quality time
6:00 Dinner
6:45 Clear table, stack dishes in kitchen. Brush teeth
7:00 Keyboard practice
7:30 Homework
9:00 Pack school bag for tomorrow
9:10 Wash. Get ready for bed. Brush teeth
9:30 Bedtime

Jack looked at the clock and found that it was only 7:15. So right now he was supposed to be doing his keyboard practice. Which was pretty funny, if you thought about it. Poll was still singing. If anything, he was getting louder.

Tortuga Anna, Hellfire Drake,
Hanged by the neck for Morgan's sake,
Captain Kelso lost at sea,
All for Morgan's treachery.

Some more Yo ho hos followed, then a final chorus, a repeat of the final chorus, and, at last, Poll finished with a piercing screech. He sat back, apparently satisfied, and fluffed out his feathers. "Well, shipmate," he said, "that's the whole story. That's what happened."

"What?" asked Jack, his ears still ringing from the unexpected concert.

"That's the whole story. The story of Blackstrap Morgan's treachery. The story of the Curse. So now you know what to expect." Poll gave a cluck like a chicken, and added, "Shiver me timbers, shipmate. With Hellfire Drake and Tortuga Anna after you, you need to know what's going to happen, so you can get ready. Not to mention Captain Kelso, that monstrous, bloodthirsty man. I'll give you the truth of it, even the other pirates had a mortal fear of him."

Jack had a sinking feeling that he should have paid more attention to the song. How was he to know he should have been listening? If anything, it had been more a case of trying *not* to listen. His head was still throbbing.

Anyway, he told himself, that was all ancient history. He didn't care what had happened three hundred years ago. What mattered was now. And tomorrow. What if he had to fight an angry pirate?

"Poll . . . ," he said nervously, "Poll, I can't fight anyone."

"Ha ha ha," Poll laughed. "Shipmate, listening to you, a body wouldn't think you were descended from old Blackstrap Morgan. Can't fight, by thunder? You've Blackstrap's blood in your veins, lad. O' course you can fight."

Jack opened his mouth to argue with this—to say that, in fact, he couldn't fight at all, he couldn't even punch properly—when the bedroom door banged open and Rachel marched in.

"Hey there," she said. "I could hear your practice from my house, so I came over. What's going on? I saw your mom in the hallway. She's really freaked out about something. Is she going crazy? She kept talking about a parrot. And a family curse. You never told me about any curse. Is this the parrot? I guess this is the parrot."

"Yes, this is the parrot," said Jack resignedly. "Poll, Rachel. Rachel, Poll."

"Charmed," said Poll, charmingly.

"Wow. Where did you come from? Can you really talk? That's amazing. I mean, really. Nice to meet you. Are you the curse?" Rachel turned to Jack. "Why didn't you ever tell me there was a curse? This is to do with what happened at Food Quick today, right?"

"Yep," said Jack. "And I didn't tell you about it because I didn't know. Apparently everyone else knew. Mom knew. I think Dad knew. Poll knows all about it. But not me. I didn't know anything. To me, the whole thing is a big surprise." *And not one of those good surprises,* he thought to himself. "Apparently," he went on, and as he said it aloud for the first time, he realized how impossible it sounded, "some dead pirates are coming to get me."

Rachel giggled. "Right," she said.

"No, really. Dead pirates."

"Seriously?" Rachel turned back to Poll. "For real?"

"True as ever was," said Poll. "That's the Curse. Hellfire Drake, Tortuga Anna, and Captain Kelso. And the rest of the crew."

Hearing the three names again, Jack felt a cold prickling at the back of his neck.

"But why?" Rachel asked. "I mean, no offense, Jack, but why you?"

"Jack is the tenth direct descendant of Blackstrap Morgan," said Poll in an impressive voice. "Terror of the South Seas, Traitor to the Brethren—"

"No, he's not," interrupted Rachel decidedly. "He can't be."

"What?" said Jack.

Poll looked annoyed. Clearly he didn't like being interrupted.

"If this curse comes from Jack's mom's family, then his mom's the direct descendant, isn't she?" said Rachel. Jack recognized the glint in her eyes. Rachel loved an argument, and she usually won.

"Well," said Poll awkwardly, "Jack's not the *most* direct, no. But his mother is not—"

"Maybe she's not quite *male* enough, is that it?" suggested Rachel.

Poll nodded slightly. He muttered something about different times, different rules, a long time ago. Jack thought that he might be blushing under his feathers, if parrots could blush.

"Ha! Sexist," stated Rachel triumphantly. "I thought so. This is a sexist curse, Jack. You should refuse to have anything to do with it. That's the end of this curse. So there!"

"I don't suppose it works like that," said Jack. How nice that would be, to have nothing to do with this. To go back a few hours, cancel out the frightening pirate in Food Quick and the strange parrot, and follow the normal schedule for a Wednesday night.

"So how *does* it work?" asked Rachel, plunking herself down on the bed. "How do you fit in, Poll? I mean, you're not part of the curse, are you? You're on Jack's side."

"Well, to tell the truth of it," said Poll, "I was the ship's parrot on the *Neptune*. I was there the day the Curse was made, perched atop the gallows at Port Royal. But I was standing too close, and the edge of the Curse caught me. One minute, ship's parrot, 'Pieces of eight, Pieces of eight,'—no conversation, shipmates; the next minute, flung across the world to watch every one of Blackstrap's descendants—"

"Male descendants," said Rachel firmly.

Poll bowed. "Indeed. His male descendants fight the Curse. A son, a son, a grandson, a nephew . . . Down the family to Mungo Morgan, and now to Jack here. And a mighty powerful fighter he will be, by thunder."

If Jack wasn't feeling so nervous, he'd have laughed. Him, a powerful fighter? He couldn't fight pirates. He was good at math; he was good at swimming. He was okay on the keyboard, but nothing special. He liked art. None of this sounded any use at all for fighting pirates. What could he have done at Food Quick this afternoon if Stewart had jumped the counter and attacked him—hit him with a pink donut?

Still, thought Jack hopefully, maybe Mom would work it out and he wouldn't have to fight anyone.

# CHAPTER 4

That night, Jack had strange and frightening dreams, but when he woke up all he could remember were a burning smell and a loud, scary laugh that sounded like big rocks being thrown into a metal Dumpster.

He rolled sleepily out of bed and grabbed his school sweater to put on over his pajamas. The night before, Poll had made a number of rude and witty comments about Jack's nightwear. Maybe the pajama top was a bit childish, Jack admitted to himself. It had a picture of a rocket ship on the front, with a smiling astronaut and some little green aliens. For the moment, Jack intended to cover it up with his sweater. In the longer term, he was determined to get a plain top. Or one with a picture of a strangled parrot.

He looked over to the desk lamp, where Poll had spent the night, head tucked under his wing, but the parrot was gone. Maybe he was gone for good, thought Jack. Maybe Mom had gotten rid of the curse overnight.

But Poll was in the kitchen, perched on the back of one of the chairs, in the middle of telling some story. He had a piece of fried bread in one foot and he was waving it around.

". . . walked the plank, by the powers, in his underwear," he was saying. "And a shark took him, but spat him out again. The taste, by thunder. Three months of whale blubber, and even the sharks didn't want him, ha ha ha."

Neither Mom nor Dad were listening. Mom was frying bacon and eggs in a pan, phone clamped to her ear, concentrating. Jack noticed all her hair was standing up, and she was still wearing the same clothes as the night before. Dad was reading *Dentistry Today*. He was holding the magazine up so high that Jack could see only the top of his head. That part of him did not look happy. On the front of the magazine, however, there was a photo of a big smiling mouth, with two rows of perfect, gleaming white teeth. This big grin gave Dad a deceptively cheerful appearance. He had a bowl of bran and a cup of black coffee on the table in front of him. His hair was wet. Had he been swimming laps already this morning?

Poll noticed Jack, broke off his story in mid-sentence, and gave a screech of welcome. "Shipmate!" he said. "Seven bells of the morning watch. Half the day gone."

"It's only seven-thirty," said Jack, sliding into his chair.

"Morning, darling," said Mom, holding her hand over the phone. She flipped a fried egg, a piece of bacon, and a grilled tomato onto a plate, and put it in front of Jack. It smelled delicious.

Dad cleared his throat in an obvious kind of way, took a spoonful of bran, and chewed it pointedly. He flicked over a page of *Dentistry Today* and held it up again. Jack realized that Dad was holding the magazine in this strange way so he wouldn't have to look at Poll.

"Eat up, shipmate," said Poll, waving his bit of bread at Jack, "and we'll fetch a course for school. I've a notion to get myself some education."

Jack choked on a mouthful of orange juice. "What?" he spluttered messily. "You're coming to school with me?"

"Where you go, I go," said Poll graciously, as

if he were granting Jack a favor. "What will our studies be today? Geography, Navigation, Astronomy? Tactics of the Great Sea Battles of History? I have a monstrous love of learning, shipmate."

Mom gave up on the phone call with a sigh, sat down, and started to eat. "Voodoo priest in Haiti," she said, with her mouth full. "Expert on curses and such, but he put me on hold." She ate another big forkful of fried food. "Thought we'd have a fry-up for a change," she said, chewing. "On the phone all night. Talked to everyone. Haven't gotten anywhere yet. But don't worry. We'll get to the bottom of this. For today, it seems to me, you'll be safer at school." She took another bite and went on, "That way, if anyone turns into a pirate and tries to attack you, there'll be lots of other people around. And if it does happen, just run for help. And call me, immediately."

Poll choked on his toast. "Run for help?" he mimicked, in Mom's voice. "Blackstrap's descendant? I calculate you're a—"

"Quiet," snapped Mom, giving him a look.

Poll snorted, but didn't say anything.

"I've called the school about him." Mom indicated Poll with her fork. "They say he can go with you, if he's quiet and not disruptive at all. I did think of keeping him at home, but I decided you'll be better off with him. He knows what's going on, anyway." She sounded a bit doubtful. "In the meantime, I'll sort this out." She picked up the phone again and pressed a long series of numbers.

Dad made a noise that sounded like "Ha!" and abruptly got up from the table. He banged his breakfast dishes into the sink. "Right," he said. "Quiet. Ha!" He picked up his briefcase and stuffed *Dentistry Today* inside. "Not disruptive." As he left the kitchen, he gave a last "Ha!" over his shoulder.

Jack felt very conspicuous, walking out the front door with a bright green parrot riding on top of his head.

This morning, there was a warmish breeze, and an exotic, salty smell in the air, a mixture of the sea, spicy cooking, and ripe fruit. A large, brilliant-blue butterfly flapped by. Jack stared at it in surprise. It was twice as big as any butterfly he had ever seen—as big as a blackbird.

Jack asked Poll about the curse and what he should expect.

"Hellfire Drake'll be the first, most likely, shipmate," said Poll. "A terrible man. A giant. Chest like a barrel. He used to tie firecrackers into his beard and light them, to scare his enemies." He gave an excited screech. His claws gripped more tightly onto Jack's hair. Clearly, Poll felt ready for anything. Jack wished he, too, was feeling like that, and not as if he had just swallowed a large, cold stone. He remembered his frightening dream about the burning smell and the horrible laughter.

"What does he look like?" he asked nervously.

"Huge red beard, shipmate. Crooked teeth. Great big sea boots. And a curved sword."

Rachel was waiting at her gate, waving to them. "Come on," she called. "Morning Jack, morning Poll. Are you coming to school, Poll? They'll go nuts about that, probably. Isn't the weather weird? Is this part of the curse? I've been waiting for ages. Thought you might not be coming."

"Hi," said Jack.

"Morning, shipmate," said Poll cheerfully.

They set off down the street to school. Jack was happy to have Rachel's company this morning. Everyone they passed stared at him. A small group of high school students waiting at a bus stop on the opposite side of the street were pointing and giggling. *Anyone would think they'd never seen a parrot before,* thought Jack miserably. Still, at least they weren't turning into pirates and trying to kill him. That was something.

"Mrs. Lemon will go mental about Poll," predicted Rachel. "Remember when Sara wore those bracelets? And you know what she's like about Seth's hair. Which reminds me . . ." She started to untie the hot pink ribbons from the ends of her braids, stuffing them into her pocket.

"Poll's not really a uniform issue, though," said Jack.

"Maybe if he was gray, it'd be better," said Rachel. "You know, the school color. You can get gray parrots." She looked critically at Poll.

Poll fluffed himself up. "Folk say those gray parrots are good talkers," he said scornfully. "Ha!"

Jack couldn't imagine a gray parrot would be a better talker than Poll. "Just stay quiet in class," he pleaded. "No talking, no singing, none of that. Mrs. Lemon's really strict. I'll get in trouble." He didn't know why he was bothering with this. He felt like he had more important things to worry about.

"What sort of trouble, shipmate?" asked Poll with interest. He climbed forward on Jack's head and hung upside down, so he could look him in the face. "Keelhauling? Walking the plank? Clapping in irons? Or will she use the cat?"

"No, nothing like that," said Jack, a bit taken aback. "Just, you know, sarcasm. Shouting. Detention." Poll looked unimpressed, and Jack didn't really blame him. Compared to walking the plank, sarcasm and shouting didn't sound very tough. "All the same," he said, "you'll behave, won't you?"

"We'll see, shipmate," said Poll, not very reassuringly.

Jack and Rachel exchanged a look. It was true that Mrs. Lemon didn't keelhaul students in her class, or clap them in irons. But she was the strictest teacher in the whole school. It was unlikely that she would welcome a talking parrot into her well-ordered classroom. Jack sighed. One more problem. Not only might pirates be attacking him today, Mrs. Lemon would be too.

Just as they turned the corner toward the school, a huge bird flew overhead. It was like a seagull, but much, much bigger. Breathtakingly big. It had long, narrow wings, far longer than any bird Jack had seen before. Despite its huge size, it flew effortlessly, with only tiny movements of wings and tail. It was big enough, and strange enough, to silence even Rachel.

"Albatross," Poll informed them.

They watched silently as the huge bird glided elegantly above the street and disappeared from view behind some buildings.

"Wow," said Rachel.

Jack said nothing, but a shiver ran all the way down his spine. Surely albatrosses lived far out at sea, following ships and sea winds. Isn't that what they said on those nature documentaries? It was an eerie sight, and it seemed ominous. He felt that this was probably not a good sign . . .

CHAPTER 5

There was a small crowd of kids and parents milling around outside the classroom as usual. Jack and Rachel threaded their way through, Jack trying to ignore the pointing fingers and comments. People began to gather around him.

"How cute," said someone's mom. "Does it talk?"

"Go on," a father said to Poll. "Say something. Polly want a cracker? Polly want a cracker?"

"Hello Cocky, hello Cocky, hello Cocky," said someone else, in a croaky parrot voice.

Poll gave an angry screech. Jack reached up and grabbed him. Poll struggled and tried to flap his wings. Even though the nine o'clock bell hadn't rung yet, Jack shoved his way through the crowd and into the classroom. Rachel followed close behind. Jack could hear Poll muttering "Hello Cocky" to himself in an offended and angry kind of way.

"I'll give them Hello Cocky," the parrot said

angrily. "The scurvy lubbers. The bilge rats. Come on, shipmate. We'll take 'em on between us. Let's get out there."

"No, no, no," said Jack, keeping a firm hold of Poll. "Behave yourself."

"Let go of me, shipmate," screeched Poll. "Hello Cocky? Hello bite on the butt!"

"Please, Poll . . . ," said Jack, a bit desperately.

Suddenly, there was a chilling sound. "Shhhh." Everyone froze, even Poll. No one could say "Shhhh" like Mrs. Lemon. It sounded like tearing paper, but scary. Still holding Poll, Jack turned slowly around to face the front of the classroom.

There were kids scattered around the room, all silently staring at Jack and Poll. At the desk stood Mrs. Lemon, and she looked furious. She was a tall, bony teacher, with puffy light yellow hair, which was set solid so it never moved, not even on really windy days. Her eyes were cold and gray, and she always wore a gray jacket and skirt. When she was angry, her lips went very thin and tight, and her eyes narrowed. They were narrow now.

"What is the meaning of this?" she asked

44

through her tight, thin lips. "Jack Jones. Rachel Marconi. How dare you cause such a commotion in my classroom?"

"Sorry, Mrs. Lemon," muttered Jack and Rachel together.

"I should hope so," said Mrs. Lemon. "Kindly move in a quiet and orderly fashion to your desks. I will have no more of this undisciplined behavior." Jack and Rachel exchanged a quick glance as they went to their desks, sat down, and in a quiet and orderly fashion started to unpack their school bags. Even Poll was quiet, except for an angry "Hello Cocky" under his breath, which Mrs. Lemon chose to ignore. She stood at her desk and surveyed her silent classroom.

"And Jack," she said.

"Yes, Mrs. Lemon?" said Jack, looking up from his desk.

"If that bird"—Mrs. Lemon pointed one thin finger at Poll—"causes any more disgraceful scenes, it will be locked in a cage in the janitor's closet until the end of the day. Is that clear?"

"Yes, Mrs. Lemon," said Jack. He waited until

the teacher was distracted by someone else, then whispered to Poll, "She means it. You'd better be quiet." Poll looked thoughtful.

Mrs. Lemon liked everyone to be arranged in alphabetical order. Jack and Rachel, who were not next to each other in the alphabet, sat on different sides of the room. Jack's desk was next to the window. The desks were lined up in very precise, straight rows. The classroom was decorated with lists of the official school rules, and extra rules just for Mrs. Lemon's class. There was a platform at the front, where she could stand and look over the classroom. There was a row of computers at the back.

Jack finished taking his books from his school bag and piled them onto his desk. The room was very quiet, just shuffling noises, a few footsteps, and quiet conversation. Suddenly, Jack heard a creaking noise. He had the strange sensation that the classroom had tipped very slightly to one side. He looked up. Everything seemed normal, but a few other people were also looking around in surprise. Some of the lists of rules on the bulletin boards were flapping gently. There was another creak, and the classroom seemed to right itself. The lists of rules were still. Glancing out of the window, Jack noticed the huge albatross once more, flying overhead in a brilliant blue sky.

More kids filed into the classroom. Some were talking and laughing loudly, but Mrs. Lemon soon stopped that. A few of them spotted Poll perched on Jack's head. There was whispering, giggling, and pointing.

The bell rang.

"Go to your desks," instructed Mrs. Lemon. At the start of the year, kids had arrived late for class, had worn things that were not part of the school uniform, had made jokes, shouted, laughed, even thrown things around the classroom. But not anymore. They had been in Mrs. Lemon's class for half a year. People talked quietly, wore the correct school uniform, handed in their homework, and arrived on time. As the echoes of the nine o'clock bell died away, everyone was sitting at their desks.

"Good morning, class," said Mrs. Lemon.

"Good morning, Mrs. Lemon," said the class.

"Before we start today, I have a few announcements," said Mrs. Lemon, reading from a piece of paper. "First, there will be no swimming this afternoon. Mr. Stockton says the pool is closed today because . . ." She looked closely at the paper. "Well, it says here there is a shark in the pool." There were a few gasps and stifled giggles around the classroom. Mrs. Lemon looked stern. "Clearly some undisciplined prank," she said. "Or a typing error," she added.

Jack knew the shark was not a typing error. He looked out of the window again. The albatross was not in sight this time, but there was a small flock of seagulls in the distance, the wind was picking up, and the treetops were waving. There was another creak, and again the classroom seemed to tip slightly, as if it were floating gently on the sea.

"He's coming," whispered Poll. Jack swallowed.

"Now," Mrs. Lemon went on, glaring. "This morning, we have a new addition to the class." She pointed at Poll. Heads turned. "Hmmph," sniffed the teacher disapprovingly. "In my opinion, a classroom is no place for a wild bird. So one false move—" She broke off, mid-sentence, as if she had forgotten what she was going to say. She shook her head slightly, and repeated, "One false move . . ."

Again, she stopped. Then she shuddered visibly. Her arms made a few strange flapping movements. The class was silent. Everyone was staring. "One false move . . ." This time, her voice was much deeper and louder.

"Ha ha ha ha!" she laughed suddenly. The laugh was shockingly loud. There were some frightened gasps. No one had heard Mrs. Lemon laugh before, and certainly not like that. Something was happening to her. Incredible as it seemed, Mrs. Lemon was growing. And swelling. Her face was changing, spreading sideways, becoming lumpier. Her puffy yellow hair was flattening and turning a rusty red color. More hair was sprouting from her chin, quickly thickening into a bushy beard. Her arms and legs were jerking around. Her sensible shoes flipped off. It was horrifying.

One of the girls screamed. Poll gave a sudden screech. The people at the front desks scrambled to their feet and backed away.

Mrs. Lemon's gray jacket and skirt stretched tighter and tighter over her huge new body.

Buttons popped off the front of her jacket and the seams started to burst apart.

Now she was as big as a gorilla, with a chest like a hairy barrel and arms like tree trunks with bulging muscles.

There was a smell of burning. Her head was surrounded by smoke. There were sparks and sizzling noises in her bushy red beard. She laughed again. "Ha ha ha ha!" It was deafening.

She tried to take a step and, for a moment, her huge new legs were pinned together by the ragged remains of her skirt. Then the skirt seemed to dissolve into the air. All at once, the teacher was wearing a pair of stained, frayed pants, a leather vest, and enormous boots.

The classroom gave a creak and rocked to one side. More people started to scream. Someone got the door open and kids fought to get out. Mrs. Lemon strode up and down the platform, stamping her boots, laughing, and watching the panic. The classroom tipped back, with a creaking groan, and started to tilt the other way. Mrs. Lemon kept her feet easily, but some of the kids fell over, and the desks started to slide across the floor. Mrs. Lemon laughed again and slapped her huge thigh with a sharp-looking, curved sword that she was suddenly holding.

"Jack Morgan," she thundered. Jack felt his heart lurch with panic. He took a quick look around. Some kids were standing frozen, bug-eyed and gaping. Rachel was looking pale and frightened. Everyone else was fleeing out the door. The classroom was rocking slowly from side to side, creaking and groaning. Poll was still riding on Jack's head, hanging on tight and giving an occasional excited screech.

"Jack Morgan," shouted Mrs. Lemon again. But, of course, this wasn't Mrs. Lemon anymore, thought Jack. This was Hellfire Drake. This was the Curse.

"Jack Morgan," shouted Hellfire Drake, fixing his glare onto Jack and grinning in a scary way, showing crooked yellow teeth. "Blackstrap's brat. There you be."

Poll screeched again, flapping his wings. "Do your worst, Hellfire," he shrieked.

"Arrrrgh!" roared Hellfire Drake. He slashed the curved sword viciously through the air.

"Blackstrap's brat and Blackstrap's parrot." He stepped off the platform and stamped down the classroom toward Jack. "All you other scurvy rats, make sail!" he shouted. The last few kids scrambled to the door and disappeared outside.

"Run, Rachel," called Jack, backing away from the huge pirate.

"No way," said Rachel bravely, trying to keep her feet as the classroom heaved and rocked from side to side.

Hellfire Drake bellowed over his shoulder, "If you stay, wench, you'll be sharks' breakfast." He turned back to Jack and stamped closer. He flicked a desk out of his way as if it were made of paper. It flew across the room and smashed to splinters against the wall. Jack backed up some more. The classroom lurched. Hellfire Drake sliced a desk in half with his sword. He trampled the bits of desk under his huge boots. Jack gulped, took a few more steps backward, and came up against one of the computer tables at the back of the room.

Hellfire Drake stamped toward him, roared, lifted the sword high above his head, and brought it swishing down. Jack dived desperately aside. Poll screeched and flew upward. The sword hit the computer and sliced through the keyboard. It buried itself into the floor only millimeters from Jack's feet.

Jack rolled away, his feet tingling from the near miss. He jumped up and ran as fast as he could across the rocking floor, dodging overturned chairs and broken desks.

Hellfire Drake grunted as he wrenched his sword out of the floorboards. "Ha ha ha," he thundered, stamping after Jack. "Run, run as fast as you can, Blackstrap's brat."

His heart pounding, Jack ducked and weaved and zigzagged around the classroom. Hellfire Drake was huge and frighteningly strong, but Jack was faster. Crash, smash, Jack ducked a flying desk and swerved to avoid the slashing sword blade.

Poll flew overhead screaming and cursing. "Hellfire, let's see you fight," he screamed. "You hairy lubber. Rot in Davy Jones's locker."

The small part of Jack's brain that was not concentrating on running away took a moment to wish that Poll would shut up. He dived under a desk and came out the other side, just as it was sliced into two pieces and then stamped to firewood. He quickly jumped over a fallen chair. He zigzagged between some desks. Hellfire Drake merely kicked things out of his way or crushed them underfoot.

Jack risked a glance over his shoulder, and as he did, his foot caught on the leg of a broken desk. The desk toppled sideways. Jack felt a stabbing pain as his ankle twisted. The desk fell across his foot, trapping it. Jack fell, hard, onto the floor. He struggled to get up, but it was no use. There was an overturned chair at his back, and his foot was pinned by the splintered desk. He looked up.

Hellfire Drake was looming above him, laughing. His eyes were bright, and his beard was crackling and sparking. He lifted his huge sword high in the air. Jack closed his eyes. *This is the end,* he thought.

CHAPTER 6

With his eyes shut, and trembling with fear, Jack waited helplessly for the curved sword to come slicing down. Instead, he heard a thump. He opened his eyes. Hellfire Drake was looking slightly stunned, the sword hanging limply from his huge, hairy hand. After a bewildered moment, Jack saw what had happened. Rachel had climbed up on a desk behind the pirate, carrying a chair. The thump had been the chair crashing down on top of his enormous head. Although it was only a plastic chair, it had metal legs—and it must have hurt. Hellfire Drake bellowed with pain and turned around. Rachel had already jumped off the desk and was halfway across the classroom. The hairy, smoldering pirate laughed loudly and, leaving Jack unsliced, stamped after Rachel.

Jack tugged at his trapped foot. Pain shot up his leg, but he had to get free. He couldn't just wait here, stuck, until Hellfire Drake finished chopping up Rachel and came back to Jack for more slicing and dicing. He had to do something. He had to save them both. He shoved the broken desk with one hand, grabbed his ankle with the other, gritted his teeth, waited for the classroom to tip the right way, and pulled.

There was a sharp stab of pain. "Owww," yelled Jack. He pulled again, trying to ignore the pain. He pulled harder, and his foot squeezed agonizingly under the edge of the desk and came free. He gasped with relief and scrambled upright.

He hobbled a few steps and found he had twisted his ankle so badly that he could hardly put his foot on the ground. It was tricky to keep his balance at all, with the classroom now lurching drunkenly from side to side. How could he stop Hellfire Drake when he couldn't even walk? The pirate was so big and so strong. All Jack had was his brain. *So think!* he said to himself.

He stared fiercely at Hellfire Drake and desperately tried to think of a plan. The pirate was still chasing Rachel. He was still laughing. His beard was still sparking and smoking. Jack looked quickly around the room. It was chaos—

everything seemed to be either overturned or smashed to pieces. Mrs. Lemon wouldn't like this at all. Thinking about Mrs. Lemon gave Jack an idea.

"Poll!" he called. Poll had been circling the room, screeching with excitement. He flew down and landed on Jack's head.

"Shipmate!"

"Poll," said Jack urgently. "Where is Mrs. Lemon? Is she still in there?" He pointed at Hellfire Drake, who had cornered Rachel and was waving his sword menacingly.

"She's in there," said Poll. "When Hellfire goes, she'll be back."

"Right," said Jack determinedly. He limped a few steps toward the pirate and called out, "Mrs. Lemon. Hey, Mrs. Lemon!"

Hellfire Drake's huge head turned toward him. His beady eyes gleamed. "Arrrgggh!" he bellowed.

"Mrs. Lemon," called Jack again. "I haven't done my homework. And do you know what? I'm not going to!"

Hellfire Drake roared again, left Rachel, and started to stomp toward Jack.

"Mrs. Lemon," Jack cried, trying to keep his balance on the shifting floor. "Look at my uniform. All ripped and dirty. Look at this." One of Jack's shirt sleeves was torn and hanging loose. He grabbed the hanging piece, ripped it off completely, and waved it at the approaching pirate.

Hellfire Drake shook with laughter. He towered above Jack. "Blackstrap's brat," he thundered, waving his sword. "Ha ha ha. Chop chop chop."

"Look, look, Mrs. Lemon," said Jack, trying to keep his voice steady. "Look at all the desks, all smashed. We're completely out of control, Mrs. Lemon." Was she inside there still? Could she hear him? "Mrs. Lemon!" he yelled.

Still laughing, Hellfire Drake lifted his sword. Jack struggled to keep upright on one foot as the classroom tipped again. He was losing hope.

"Mrs. Lemon," he said despairingly, looking up at the sharp blade. This was it.

"Mrs. Lemon," came Rachel's voice. "Over here. Look at me!"

Hellfire Drake turned. Rachel was standing on a broken desk. She had tied the pink ribbons back onto the ends of her braids, and she was holding them out.

Go, Rachel, thought Jack. *That's the idea.* But would it work?

The pirate roared again. Was there a faint coldness in his tone? A hint of Mrs. Lemon? And was he shrinking slightly? Jack thought so. He hoped so.

"Look, Mrs. Lemon," Rachel called, in a taunting, singsong voice designed to irritate any teacher. "Pretty pink ribbons. Aren't they beautiful?"

Now the pirate was definitely shrinking. It was as if Mrs. Lemon had stirred to life inside him at the sight of the pink ribbons and was fighting to take over. The arms flapped, the legs jerked, the head wobbled from side to side.

From behind, Jack could see the huge body deflating. The bushy red hair was fading to yellow and puffing up. Rachel kept talking about her pink ribbons, how nice they were, how pink. Hellfire Drake gave one last roar. It was faint and weak. To Jack, it sounded funny, as if Mrs. Lemon was trying to do a pirate imitation.

He started to giggle. He couldn't help it. He collapsed down onto the floor. Poll lost his balance, gave a surprised screech, and flew off. Jack leaned his back against an overturned desk and laughed and laughed.

When Jack looked up, the only thing left of Hellfire Drake was the faint haze of smoke around Mrs. Lemon's head. Jack had never thought he would be happy to see Mrs. Lemon, but he was happy now. She might be strict, but she had never chased after him waving a sharp sword and laughing like a maniac. The classroom had stopped rocking as if it were riding the waves of a stormy sea, and it had settled down to rest on solid ground again. Jack wiped his eyes and got clumsily to his feet—or to one of his feet, at least.

Mrs. Lemon was looking shaky and confused. She was wearing her gray jacket and skirt again, but they were ripped and ragged and streaked with scorch marks. Her gaze settled on Rachel. "Rachel Marconi," she said in a weak voice.

"Oh, Mrs. Lemon," said Rachel, sounding relieved and exhausted.

"What do you think you are wearing in your hair?" asked Mrs. Lemon. She seemed to be speaking automatically, not as if she really meant it. "Remove those items this instant. Kindly consult the school rules and write out the section concerning uniform. In your best handwriting."

"Yes, Mrs. Lemon," said Rachel resignedly, untying the ribbons. "But—"

"What has been happening in this classroom?"asked Mrs. Lemon, looking around vaguely. She spotted Jack. "Jack Jones. Look at the state of you. You, also, may consult the school rules, and write out that same section."

"Yes, Mrs. Lemon," said Jack, feeling a bit less pleased that she was back. "But Mrs. Lemon—"

"Where is the rest of the class? Look at this classroom. You two, start to put this room back into some sort of order. Silence that screeching bird. I seem to be suffering from a headache."

That would be from Rachel bashing you over the head with a chair, thought Jack.

"Where is the rest of the class?" Dazed, Mrs. Lemon looked around and then down at herself. She froze in shock and then gasped. "What?" She wrapped her arms around herself, said a surprisingly rude word, and ran from the room.

Jack couldn't help laughing. He had never thought he would see Mrs. Lemon in such a state. And she obviously had no memory of being inside Hellfire Drake.

Poll flew down and landed on Jack's head. "A bracing little battle, by thunder," he said. "I give you joy, shipmate. A mighty pretty fight."

"No thanks to you," said Jack. Now that it was all over, he was feeling fairly good, apart from his ankle, and pleased with himself. He exchanged a grin with Rachel.

"Ha ha ha," said Poll. "You fight the Curse, shipmate, not me. You did well, though. Hellfire wasn't expecting that. You had the weather gauge of him. He'll be a sight more careful of you next time around."

"Next time?" asked Jack in alarm.

"Mind, he'll wait a few days, to be sure," Poll said cheerfully. "Most likely, Tortuga Anna'll be sailing in before then. Folk called her the Black Widow because of the way she moved, like a spider. Deadly, shipmates. She could throw a knife twenty feet, either hand, you'd only feel the wind as it went by, and you'd have a new haircut and no buttons on your coat, ha ha ha."

"Oh," said Jack glumly, feeling very tired all of a sudden. He sank down onto the floor again.

By now, the rest of the class had started to trickle back into the room. Many of them still looked shocked. There was a nervous atmosphere. People were talking too loudly, laughing suddenly for no reason, and jumping like frightened grasshoppers when anyone came up behind them.

Someone said they had seen Mrs. Lemon race to her car and drive off very fast. "All her clothes were ripped to pieces."

"And you should've heard what she was saying!" said Sara, then went on to tell them. The rest of the class was impressed by Mrs. Lemon's vocabulary.

"What *was* that anyway?" people asked Jack and Rachel.

"What happened to her?"

'That was so weird. Scary. What happened?"

"Why was she calling you Jack Morgan?"

"Yeah. You're Jack Jones. Who's Jack Morgan?"

Before Jack and Rachel could explain what had happened—although Jack felt this would probably be impossible anyway—there was a sound from outside that made everyone in the classroom stop talking and turn anxiously toward the door. The sound was very familiar, faint but getting louder.

"Oh no," said someone gloomily.

"One, Two, One, Two, One, Two, One, Two . . ." came the sound.

Someone said one of the rude words that Mrs. Lemon had used.

"One, Two, One, Two, One, Two, Mor, Ning, Mor, Ning . . ." Into the class jogged the short, solid sports teacher, Mr. Stockton. Everyone groaned. Mr. Stockton jogged up onto the platform, jogged briskly over to the teacher's desk, and jogged around it several times. He lifted his knees up very high and counted loudly, "One, Two, One, Two . . ."

After a minute or two, he stopped jogging and started doing jumping jacks. "Come, On, Every, One," he shouted in time to his jumping. "Jumping, Jacks, Every, One, One, Two, One, Two . . ." A few people joined in halfheartedly, but most of the class was still feeling too shattered to jump around. Jack couldn't put his injured foot on the ground at all. Rachel made no move to get up. But Poll clucked happily and jumped along in time to the teacher, flapping his wings.

"Touch, Toes, Touch, Toes," shouted Mr. Stockton, doing just that. "Up, Down, Up, Down." He did a few more toe touches, and then some side stretches, finishing with some arm circles, both arms, both ways, before finally blowing his whistle and coming to a stop.

"Morning, morning," he said crisply, not even breathing heavily. "This class is in big trouble. Terrible. All the desks smashed. Never seen such terrible behavior. Detentions forever. Mrs. Lemon had to go home, so I'm here instead. Morning: math. Afternoon: cross-country run. Right? Right." He looked around at the mainly unenthusiastic faces and spotted Poll. "A parrot," he said. "Whose parrot? Your parrot?"

"Well, I guess," said Jack, not sure if Poll was exactly his.

"My own parrot," said Poll, sounding a bit put out. "But I'm with young Jack here. I am the Pirate Curse. Or, at least, part of it."

Mr. Stockton clearly didn't understand this at all. "A talking parrot," he said. "Excellent. Had a pet once. Dog. Greyhound. Had to get rid of it. Couldn't keep up with me." He looked closely at Jack. "Bad leg? Hamstring?"

"I twisted my ankle,"admitted Jack.

"School nurse," instructed Mr. Stockton. "Go now. The rest, follow me. Do math and jog around the school. Best way to learn. Maintenance will fix this disgraceful mess. Come on, One, Two, One, Two, One, Two, Three, Four . . ." He jogged out of the room. The rest of the class trailed slowly after him. Rachel pulled a face at Jack over her shoulder as she trotted away with the others.

Jack limped slowly off to see the school nurse, and to call his mom to tell her what had happened. Poll, riding on his head, shouted "One, Two, One, Two," encouragingly. It was very irritating.

CHAPTER 7

Jack was exhausted. The school nurse had bandaged his ankle, but it still ached. He sat down on the bench outside his classroom to wait for Mom. There were hammering noises coming from inside, as Mr. Matt, the school maintenance worker, fixed all the broken furniture. The distant shouting of numbers could be heard coming from Mr. Stockton's jogging math class. Jack shut his eyes.

"Shipmate, you look fearfully pale, like a weevil. A tot of grog, that's what you need, mayhap. Set you back on your feet."

Jack opened his eyes to see Poll's concerned face, very close and upside down. "I'm okay. Just a bit tired," he said.

"A bolus? A tonic of some kind? Whale blubber and molasses is a powerful mixture," suggested Poll.

"No, thanks, I'm fine."

"A big slice of figgy duff. Line your stomach. Or mayhap pork fat, with cod-liver oil and seaweed, rubbed into your chest. Prodigiously medicinal."

"No, no," said Jack, feeling slightly sick.

Luckily, before Poll could continue, Mom drove into the parking lot with a squeal of tires. She jumped out of the car and looked around frantically. Jack noticed that she still hadn't changed her clothes, and her hair, which was normally sleek and neat, was standing up in weird, untidy spikes. She was wearing her fluffy purple slippers, making it hard for her to run. She managed it, though, when she spotted Jack.

"Jack, Jack," she said, engulfing him in a hug. "Darling. Oh no, look at your foot. What happened? Poll, how could you let this happen to him? You should have been taking care of him. Come on, let's go. Where's your bag?"

She grabbed Jack's arm and helped him to his feet.

"I can walk," Jack protested. "It's only twisted."

Mom didn't seem to hear. She half carried him to the car and pushed him in.

"I've taken a few days off work." She got in and started the engine. "I'm going to sort this out, so don't worry. Obviously, I was wrong about you being at school, around lots of people. My new plan is much better."

The car started with a shuddering lurch and zoomed out into the street. Poll shrieked with excitement.

"All sails set," he yelled. "Weigh anchor!"

"Ummm," Jack said anxiously. "Umm . . . so what's the new plan?"

"Isolation." Mom swerved around another car and darted back just in time to avoid a van coming the other way. "No more school until I sort out this problem. I'll lock you away from everyone. Even away from me and Dad. That'll do the trick. If you don't see anyone, then no one can turn into a pirate. That should keep you safe."

Jack didn't like the sound of this. Was Mom really planning to lock him up? She was acting very strangely. Fingers drumming on the wheel, nervous, fast talking, fluffy slippers, untidy hair. This wasn't like her at all.

Jack tried to take his mind off Mom's new scary style of driving by looking out the window. They had stopped at a red light next to a line of people waiting at a bus stop. There were a couple of elderly ladies with shopping bags, a mom with a toddler, and a man in paint-stained overalls.

Poll gave a loud screech and yelled, "Shipmate! Pirates to larboard!"

Before Jack's horrified eyes, the old ladies started to swell and grow, and within a second or two they had turned into huge pirates with bulging muscles, gold earrings, and stripey shirts. The mother changed into an enormous yellow-bearded pirate, and her toddler grew fur and a tail and ran chattering up onto her shoulder. The man in the overalls suddenly had a long pigtail hanging down his back. His bare, sunburned arms blossomed with tattoos and he was holding three short, sharp swords, one in each hand and one clamped between his crooked yellow teeth. It all happened very quickly. One second, normal bus line. Next second, four angry pirates and a monkey.

Even though Jack had already seen this same kind of thing happen to Mrs. Lemon, it was still shocking and horrifying. And very frightening.

"Mom!" he shouted.

Mom glanced over at the bus line and gasped. She stamped on the accelerator. The car jerked a couple of inches forward, coughed, and stopped. Frantically, Mom tried to start it again. Jack watched helplessly as the four pirates crept toward the car. They cracked their knuckles and snarled menacingly. The bearded pirate with the monkey bent down to look in Jack's window. The monkey bared its sharp teeth. The pirate slammed a meaty hand down onto the roof of the car. Jack yelled and ducked down in his seat.

"Jack Morgan," roared the pirate. "Come out and fight, you lubber."

Just in time, Mom got the car started. She swerved up onto the curb to avoid one of the pirates, then bumped back onto the road and shot through the intersection at the instant the lights changed to green.

Jack craned backward and saw two old ladies, a mother with a toddler, and a man in overalls standing by the side of the road, looking confused.

Poll was laughing. "Ha ha ha, they're after you now, shipmate. That was some of the crew of the *Neptune*. An honorable retreat. Next time, you'll attack, I make no doubt."

Jack leaned back in his seat. That was close.

Mom screeched into the driveway, just missing the fence by a few inches, and slammed on the brakes. She dragged Jack out of the car, through the front door, up the stairs, and into his bedroom. Poll swooped down to perch on the desk lamp.

Mom backed out of the room quickly. "Jack, you stay here," she said. "I don't want you to worry or anything, but I can't let anyone come near you. Not even me. I might turn into a pirate and try to kill you. That would be terrible. I want you to lock yourself in."

Jack looked at his bedroom door and noticed a shiny new lock, two bolts, and a security chain.

"Remember, don't let anyone in," warned Mom. "No one at all."

"Wait," said Jack. He wanted to ask: *What about food? What about the bathroom? What about my friends? What about my life? I can't spend my life locked in my bedroom.*

But Mom had already shut the door. "Come

on, Jack," she was saying from the other side. "Lock the door."

He got to his feet, and slowly turned the key in the shiny new lock. He pushed the two bolts across. He hooked up the security chain.

"And don't worry," he heard Mom's worried voice say. "I'm going to get help. I've got someone coming tomorrow who will fix everything." He heard her footsteps as she hurried downstairs. He heard the little beep as she picked up the phone.

Jack collapsed onto his bed with his hands over his face. What was Mom planning? Who was coming tomorrow? Would he ever leave his bedroom again?

A knock at the door woke him up. The late afternoon sun was slanting in through the window. He must have been asleep for hours. He yawned, feeling disoriented and confused.

There was another knock, then Rachel's voice called, "Jack, are you in there?" The door handle rattled.

"Hey, Rachel." Jack got off his bed and stumbled to the door.

"Shipmate," shrieked Poll in welcome. He flew down to the floor and screwed his head around, trying to peer under the door with one beady eye.

"Hi!" called Rachel. "Don't open the door. Your mom says you have to keep it locked. But I've got some stuff for you, and I'll slip it underneath. She says you can eat things that fit under the door. Is she all right, do you think? Here's some cheese."

Jack suddenly realized he was very hungry. He had eaten nothing since breakfast. He sat on the floor next to the door, leaning up against the end of the bed. When the slice of cheese appeared under the door, he broke it in two and gave half to Poll. Next, Rachel slid three jelly sandwiches under the door. They looked like they had been squashed flat specially to fit. Then came an apple, cut into ragged slices, some dry cookies, some more cheese, and some lettuce leaves. Last of all was a frozen fish stick. Jack and Poll ate everything. Jack was so hungry he even ate the fish stick, which was very nasty.

All the time, Rachel kept up a stream of commentary. "Jack, you're so lucky you weren't at school this afternoon. We had to run, run, run everywhere after Mr. Stockton. Math shouldn't be that exhausting, you know. I can hardly walk now. After lunch, Mrs. Lemon came back. It was amazing. I don't think she remembers anything about being a pirate. She is a bit different, though. Instead of spelling, we sang sea shanties all afternoon. She was singing and laughing. Then she did this hornpipe dance. But we have detention forever because of smashing all the desks. Which isn't exactly fair, is it? I mean, she's the one who broke everything."

Jack laughed. The thought of Mrs. Lemon dancing the hornpipe and singing sea shanties was so bizarre.

"That's the Curse," said Poll. "It takes a while to wear off."

"I thought maybe you should read this. I got it from the school library." Rachel poked a big, brightly colored book under the door. It was called *All About Pirates*. "What other things can I get you? Thin things, that is."

"Maybe I could sneak to the bathroom, if you go downstairs and keep everyone away," said Jack. "If people don't see me, then they won't turn into pirates, right? Right, Poll?"

Poll gave a cluck. "Mayhap they won't. But shipmate, whatever you do, they're going to get you. You can't run away from it."

"I'm not running away," said Jack defensively. "Mom's dealing with things. Soon everything will be worked out."

Poll snorted contemptuously.

Rachel kept guard at the bottom of the stairs so Jack could run to the bathroom and back.

After that, she said good-bye and went home to do her homework.

Jack locked himself in again, the shiny new lock, the two bolts, the security chain. He noticed Poll's expression, and said, "I'm not running away. I just don't want anyone sneaking up on me."

"You won't hear Tortuga Anna coming for you," said Poll. "You won't know she's here at all, until you look down and see your own guts all over the floor, ha ha ha. Moved like a spider, she did."

Jack began to feel sick again.

He lay on his bed and flipped through *All About Pirates*. Poll was enchanted by the pictures. He shrieked with excitement to see a map of the Caribbean. Jack leafed through the pages. Ships, Navigation, Clothing, Treasure. Weapons. He found a picture of a sword just like the one Hellfire Drake had been trying to chop him up with. *"Cutlass,"* he read. He found a picture of a pirate ship with the side cut away so all the different decks were exposed. *"Ballast,"* he read, and *"Fo'c'sle."*

He tried to ignore Poll's comments and screams of recognition. Jack didn't want to know the names of things, he wanted to know what he could do to stop a pirate from appearing and trying to kill him. Or how to get rid of a three-hundred-year-old pirate curse. The trouble with *All About Pirates* was that there was no sense of urgency in it. The pirates in the book were colorful, historical pirates, not real, angry pirates with sharp swords.

"Strangely enough," he read, *"most pirates could not swim."*

"That's the truth of it," said Poll. "Except for Captain Kelso, that monstrous man. If ever a pirate tempted fate, he did. Folk say he was in league with the devil."

At the end of the book, there was a list of famous pirates. *"Francois l'Ollonois,"* Jack read. *"One of the cruelest of buccaneers. He cut out the beating heart of a captive and chewed on it.* Gross." He looked at Poll, expecting a comment, but the parrot was transfixed by something on the opposite page.

"Captain William Kelso," Jack read, with a chill of fear. He peered at the little picture. A thin, gaunt face. Dark, dead eyes. A strange, evil smile. Jack looked closer and saw that Captain Kelso had pointed teeth, like a shark.

Poll saw the expression on Jack's face and gave an unconvincing laugh. "Shipmate, don't worry about him. You won't be meeting Captain Kelso for a good long while, by the powers. Mayhap, he won't come at all. He won't stir himself unless he has to. He'll leave the action to the others."

Jack quickly turned the page to hide Captain Kelso's evil face. Suddenly, out of the corner of his eye, he saw something move in one of the dark corners of the bedroom. He turned his head slowly and then froze in horror.

 # CHAPTER 8

Jack went stiff with fear. Every muscle in his body was tense as he stared into the shadowy corner of his bedroom. Until a moment ago, the only thing in that corner had been a balled-up pair of socks. There were no socks now. Instead, there was the biggest spider Jack had ever seen. It had a furry body like a tennis ball, and eight hairy legs, each one as thick as a marker. It was dark brown with orange stripes on the joints of its legs. It was as big as a medium-sized kitten. If he hadn't seen it happen, he wouldn't have believed it, but it was true. His socks had turned into a great big hairy spider.

Jack really hated spiders, even little ones, and this one was enormous. It had raised its two front legs ready to attack, and it was moving toward him across the carpet, its eyes gleaming. Jack tried to speak but only a strangled sound came out.

"Poll," he croaked.

Poll gave a cluck, eyeing the spider. "Tarantula," he said knowledgeably.

"Is it poisonous?" whispered Jack.

"Deadly, shipmate. Likely, it's with Tortuga Anna. I told you she was called the Black Widow." Poll didn't sound particularly worried.

"Because she *moved* like a spider, you said. Not brought huge spiders along with her."

"Well, shipmate, she was partial to tarantulas," said Poll. "Blackstrap had a ship's parrot"—he bowed modestly—"and Tortuga Anna had a ship's spider. Several, to give you the truth of it. She used to feed them rats."

Jack looked from the spider to the door, trying to judge the distance. He had to get out of the bedroom, but how could he get past the spider? First, he would have to unlock the door, and that would take a few seconds. What if it jumped at him? He tucked his bare feet under him and struggled to breathe normally.

The spider took a few menacing steps toward the bed. Jack swallowed. His throat was dry.

"Will it—," he started to say, but then he saw something move on the bedside table. Normally there was an alarm clock in the shape of a small black dog. Not anymore. Now the alarm clock was the shape of a big black spider. Jack could see the little hairs on its legs and its cluster of black, expressionless eyes. It lifted its front two legs, took a step toward Jack, and then, suddenly, it sprang.

Jack didn't wait to see where it landed. He didn't stop to think. He catapulted himself off the bed, clear over the first spider, and slammed into the door. With frantic, panicky fingers, he turned the key in the shiny new lock, pulled back both bolts, unhooked the chain, flung the door open, and ran screaming down the stairs, completely forgetting his sore ankle.

Mom spun around and dropped the phone as Jack shot into the kitchen.

"What happened?" she asked, alarmed.

"S-s-spiders," stuttered Jack, looking around the brightly lit kitchen, half expecting the salt shaker or the coffee cup on the table to sprout hairy legs. "My socks, my clock." He shuddered. He could feel imaginary spiders walking up his legs, across his shoulders, down his neck. Shivers ran up his back, and he started to shake.

Poll flew into the room, and landed on his head. The familiar grip of his claws made Jack feel a bit steadier.

"But, Jack," said Mom urgently, "you shouldn't be out here. I told you to stay in your bedroom. It's dangerous for you to be with anyone. Even me."

"I'm not going back in there," said Jack. "No way. You should have seen them—they were as big as this." He put his two hands together, with all the fingers sticking out. "Bigger. And Poll says they're poisonous."

"Deadly," confirmed Poll brightly.

Mom looked doubtful. "How did they get in?" she asked.

"They didn't get in," said Jack. "My socks turned into one spider, and my clock turned into the other. I guess they can take over things like the pirates take over people. I'm not staying in a locked room with a bunch of poisonous spiders. No way. I'll take my chances out in the open."

"That's the spirit," said Poll encouragingly. "You can't win your battles locked in your cabin, shipmate."

Mom looked around the kitchen wildly. "No," she said. "You're much safer up there. Even now, I could turn into a pirate and attack you. It's too dangerous for you to be around anyone. Much too dangerous. I can't let anything happen to you. I'll work everything out. I'll deal with this."

Jack looked at her, and for the first time he began to wonder if she really could deal with the curse. The kitchen was littered with pieces of paper covered with scrawled messages and phone numbers. Some pieces had been ripped up, others had been crumpled and then flattened out again. There was a coffee cup, but Jack couldn't help noticing that instead of coffee it seemed to be full of pudding. Since when had Mom started drinking pudding?

"No," she was saying, the words tumbling out in a very agitated way. "No, Jack. You have to go back to your bedroom. To be safe. But if things are going to turn into spiders, I'll just get rid of all the things. That's logical. Wait here."

Jack sat down at the kitchen table to wait. He heard Mom going up the stairs, and then a series of thumps and bangs, and things being violently shoved across the floor. He guessed that the spiders had turned back into the socks and the clock, or there would have been a scream by now.

Outside, he could hear faint splashes. Dad must be home from work and swimming laps again. He must have done hundreds during the last twenty-four hours.

Poll gave a cluck, hopped off Jack's head onto the table, and started wading through the pieces of paper. He poked his beak into the coffee cup and tasted the pudding. He kicked a few pieces of paper off the table, obviously bored. Suddenly, he broke into song.

"Where's my leg?" cried old Joe Pegg.
"Shot off by the Navy.
Grab ahold before it's cold,
And serve it up with gravy."

The windowpanes vibrated and the cups on the shelf rattled. Despite everything, Jack began to giggle. Mom came back down the stairs, running as fast as she could in her fluffy purple slippers, panting and slapping her hands together.

"Okay, Jack, that's done. You'll be safe up there now. Go on up and lock yourself in."

"But, Mom—" Jack really didn't want to spend any more time locked in his room.

"No, Jack. Don't argue with me. Up you go. Go on." Mom started to shuffle through the scraps of paper. She took a big swallow of pudding and made a face. "Coffee's tasting odd today. Look, Jack, I've got everything under control. Tomorrow morning, there's an expert coming who'll work everything out. A doctor. All the way from Europe. So don't worry. Everything will be fine."

Jack saw she was exhausted from lack of sleep and stress. Reluctantly, he turned and limped upstairs with Poll. On the way to his bedroom, he passed piles of his clothes and books, and his keyboard. His neatly written lists and schedules, with the different activities highlighted in different colors, lay scattered on the floor. There was his wooden box with Uncle Mungo's presents in it. And just outside his door were his dresser, his desk, and his bed. When he entered his room, he wasn't surprised to see it was completely empty. The only things in it were a sleeping bag in one corner and his folded pajamas.

Well, Mom's dealt with the spider problem, thought Jack, as he closed the door and locked all the locks. There was nothing left in the room that could turn into a tarantula. He changed into the pajamas, unrolled the sleeping bag, and crawled into it. What else was there to do in an empty room? There was nothing left for Poll to perch on for the night, so he settled on Jack's shoulder.

The shiny new locks gleamed in the light from the window, and from outside, Jack could still hear the faint splashes from the pool as Dad swam lap after lap. Was this how his life was going to be, locked in an empty bedroom eating food slid under the door? With Mom drinking pudding thinking it was coffee, and Dad swimming up and down the pool forever?

Despite his tiredness, when Jack shut his eyes he couldn't sleep. It was too uncomfortable on the floor, and the empty room was too depressing.

"Poll," he said quietly, after a few minutes.

"Shipmate?"

"Tell me about the curse. How did it start? What did Blackstrap Morgan do exactly?"

"Ah," said Poll, "the story of the Curse. Well, shipmate, there was a treasure ship, the *Santa Rosa*. Four pirate captains formed an alliance to take her: Blackstrap Morgan, Hellfire Drake, Tortuga Anna, and the Dread Captain Kelso. They sailed in Blackstrap's ship, the *Neptune,* and Captain Kelso's ship, the *Vengeance*. They took the *Santa Rosa* in a mighty battle and carried the treasure off to Skeleton Island."

"Where's that?"

"D'ye not learn geography at that school? A secret location, known only to the brotherhood of the coast. Think on this, shipmate. Thick jungle, right down to the sand. Monkeys whooping. Butterflies as big as saucers. Two pirate ships anchored in the lagoon and a pile of glittering treasure on the beach. Doubloons, shipmate. Jewels, pearls, crowns. Pieces of eight. Sovereigns. Gold ingots. All glittering in the sun . . ." He stopped for a moment, remembering.

"The council sat to divide up the treasure,

by the accord. Two shares to each captain, one share to every sailor, half a share to every boy."

"Or girl, Rachel would say," said Jack.

"She would that," agreed Poll. "Then the shares were sewn into cloth, marked, carted up to the top of the headland, and buried." He stopped.

Jack waited for the parrot to continue, but he didn't. "Then what happened?" he asked.

For the first time since he had arrived, Poll seemed reluctant to talk. Finally he said, "That night, there was a big bonfire lit on the beach. All the pirates were singing and dancing. Drinking. But the next morning, everyone was shocked from their sleep by cannon fire. There, just outside the lagoon, were four British Navy men-o'-war, firing on our ships. Pirates were running everywhere in mad confusion. 'We're fouled,' shouted Captain Kelso. 'Blackstrap's betrayed us. To me, to me!' And he ran for the boats, with some of his men. He rowed out to the *Vengeance* and set sail, but it was too late. She was holed, and she sank in deep water, at the edge of the lagoon, among the Navy ships. Captain Kelso was lost. Drowned, shipmate."

Jack could imagine the scene, pirates rowing their small boats out to the anchored ships, the Navy men-o'-war firing their cannons, the confusion, the noise.

"Soon the redcoats came ashore," Poll went on. "There was fighting in the water, on the beach, in the jungle. Many soldiers killed, many pirates. A bloody battle. It took fifteen soldiers to bring down Hellfire Drake and twenty to capture Tortuga Anna. They were taken to Port Royal in Jamaica and hanged. As was the rest of the crew."

"And Blackstrap Morgan?" asked Jack.

Poll looked sad. "That's the hard thing, shipmate. Blackstrap was not on the beach that morning. He was not there to fight. He'd betrayed the location of Skeleton Island to the British so the Navy could set up an ambush, then stole off in a small boat, mayhap, while everyone was sleeping. Taking the treasure. He was not seen again. I always thought him a good man. He always stuck to the code, never betrayed a comrade. But that black day, he sold the lives of his friends in return for treasure. An evil deed."

Jack could think of nothing to say. Betraying your friends in return for money was a terrible thing to do. One of the worst things anyone could do. And this was his own great-great-many-times-great grandfather.

"That's why he was cursed, shipmate," said Poll quietly.

Jack nodded silently. Now he understood.

CHAPTER 9

Jack woke to find hot sunshine blazing into his empty bedroom. He sat up and yawned. Poll tumbled off his shoulder. Jack stretched. He felt stiff and aching after sleeping on the floor all night. How early was it? He couldn't tell. He sat for a few minutes, thinking about the day before, half listening to Poll's grumbles as he tidied his feathers.

Looking around the sad, bare room, Jack came to a decision. He wouldn't spend the day locked up in here. No way. And he wouldn't be waiting for Mom to slip his breakfast under the door. He got up and unlocked the lock, unbolted the bolts, and unhooked the security chain. He opened the door and peered out cautiously. The hallway wasn't empty—it contained all his possessions, heaped together in untidy piles. Most important, though, it was empty of angry pirates and giant spiders.

Jack sighed with relief and quietly left the bedroom. He went first to the bathroom and then downstairs to the kitchen. His ankle was a lot better this morning, and he found he could walk almost normally again. He was starving.

Mom was fast asleep at the kitchen table, her head resting on a pile of paper. One of her hands was still clutching the phone. Dad wasn't up yet.

"Shhh," Jack said to Poll. Poor Mom, so tired from phone calls and worry. Quietly, Jack collected things for breakfast. Green soda. A package of cheese crackers and a jar of strawberry jam. Two bananas and two apples. With his arms full, he managed to unlock the back door and walk out into the yard.

It was a beautiful morning. It was already hot, and the sun was sparkling on the water in the pool. The garden seemed to have grown a lot overnight. Normally, the lawn was as neat as a carpet. Dad took great care of the lawn. This morning, though, the grass looked thick and wavy. The bushes around the lawn and the pool looked unruly and very green. Jack noticed that some vines were growing up the side of the house and tangling into the branches of the trees.

There were some new red and orange dangling flowers and one of those huge blue butterflies was flapping lazily around. Jack sat down on the bottom step, which was warm from the sun, and laid out the food. Poll gave a happy chuckle, hopped down from Jack's head, and started breakfast.

Jack dipped the cheese crackers into the jam and washed them down with green soda, something he couldn't do with either Mom or Dad watching. Poll munched up both apples, humming cheerfully to himself. After about ten minutes, Jack sat back with a contented sigh and peeled a banana.

Maybe it was just the sunshine and the delicious breakfast, but today Jack felt ready for anything.

There was the sound of a car engine in the driveway, car doors slamming, footsteps on the path, and then the front doorbell ringing. Jack heard Mom cry out in surprise. He guessed the doorbell had woken her up.

After a minute, there were muffled voices inside.

"What's this, shipmate?" asked Poll, cocking his head to the side.

Jack shrugged. Then he heard Mom calling, so he got up and went into the house.

"Jack," cried Mom. "What were you doing out there? I told you to stay in your room. Anything could have happened to you." She looked terribly anxious, and very tired. Her hair was really strange this morning, all flat on one side from sleeping on the table, and there was a paper clip clinging to the side of her face.

She reached out to Jack. "Come in here." She propelled him into the study.

In the study were two strangers wearing white coats. One was a tall, thin man with a little square-cut black beard and a shiny bald head. He was wearing thick glasses. The other was a much shorter, fatter man with a head of fluffy red hair. The fatter man was unpacking what looked like scientific instruments and computer parts from several black metal cases. He was uncoiling cables and hooking things up.

The taller man spun to look at Jack,

accidentally sweeping a pile of papers off the desk. He made a strange, jerky movement of his head. "Aha!" he said with enthusiasm, his pale eyes swimming around behind his glasses like little fish. "Hello, little boy. And parrot. Excellent. Excellent."

Hello, little boy, thought *Jack. Hello bite on the butt.*

"This is my son, Jack," said Mom to the two men. "And this is Poll. Jack, this is Doctor van Donkel." She pointed at the taller man, who wagged his head from side to side. "And Doctor Zoob." She pointed at the short, fat man, who was on his hands and knees picking up papers. He looked up and gave Jack a little wave.

Mom went on. "These doctors have come all the way from Europe, Jack, to help us. To help you. They're experts in . . . in this kind of thing."

Dad came into the study, still wearing his pajamas, rubbing his eyes. "Do you know what time it is?" he said annoyed.

Mom introduced everyone again. Dad shook hands.

"What would you like? Coffee? Tea?" asked

Mom, twisting her hands nervously. "Something to eat?"

"Yes, I would—," Doctor Zoob started to say.

"No, no, nothing at all," interrupted Doctor van Donkel, with an airy wave of his hand, which knocked a jar of pens onto the floor. The jar rolled under the desk and the pens scattered. "The thrill of scientific discovery is being sustenance enough. We are not needing food."

Doctor Zoob looked a bit disappointed to hear this.

Doctor van Donkel sat down at the desk and said, "We are starting straight away. For me, I am a hot potato with expectation, as you say. No?" He took a pad of paper from his briefcase and a pen from his top pocket and started scribbling down notes. He wrote lists of numbers, drew little graphs, circled things, and shot big arrows right across the page to join things together.

Without looking up, he said, "Be coming here, little boy." He waved a hand at the empty chair opposite, knocking a small potted cactus off the desk. It hit Doctor Zoob, who was picking up pens, on the head.

Mom gave Jack a look and jerked her head toward the chair.

Reluctantly, he went around the desk and sat down, facing the doctor.

Doctor van Donkel peered intently at Jack and Poll, and scribbled another page of notes. He said, "So, when were you first seeing these, er, pirates?"

"Umm, Wednesday, I guess. And yesterday," said Jack.

"Aha! Wonderful. Excellent. And what else are you seeing? Fairies? Aliens? Unicorns, perhaps?" Doctor van Donkel looked at Jack, his pale eyes alight with hope.

"No," said Jack. "No, just pirates."

Doctor van Donkel's face fell. "Just pirates." Then he brightened. "Still, a bird in the hand is worth two in the bath, as you say, no?"

"No," said Jack. "I mean, there's no such thing as fairies and aliens and whatever else you said. These are *real* pirates."

Doctor van Donkel looked up, jerked his head around in a disconcerting way, and said, "Oh yes," with a significant look at Doctor Zoob, who was picking cactus spines and dirt out of his hair. He wrote *Denial* down on his pad and drew a big black circle around it.

Poll screeched, his claws biting into Jack's scalp. "Avast, you lubber," he said. "That's mighty pretty. The Pirate Curse is real, by the powers. I've a notion to—"

"Poll," snapped Mom. "Be quiet."

"Ah!" said Doctor van Donkel. "Interesting. Excellent. A trained bird. Marvelous. Avipedagogy." He wrote this down.

Poll screeched angrily.

"What?" said Jack. "Poll's right. There *are* real pirates. There *is* a curse."

"Yes, yes. Excellent," said Doctor van Donkel, drawing bigger circles around *Denial* and shooting a starburst of arrows out from it.

"Jack," said Mom, "please cooperate with the doctor. He's come a long way to help you. Poll, please be quiet. But, Doctor, you do understand, don't you? This is a real problem, and there are real pirates—I've seen them myself."

"Marvelous. Interesting. A Consanguinitous Delusion," he said, scribbling so wildly his pen tore a hole in the sheet of paper.

Dad said, "Wait a minute—" but Doctor van Donkel interrupted him.

"Please, I have this already. Denial. Yes. No more denial, thank you. I have it here." He pointed a bony finger at the pad. Then he flipped over the page with a flourish, which knocked the phone off the desk, hitting Mom on the foot. "Enough denial is as good as a breakfast, as you say."

"You need to keep further away," whispered Doctor Zoob to Mom, as he picked up the phone. "He's very clever, but a bit . . . you know . . ." He waved his hands around in a Doctor van Donkel imitation.

"Where did you find him?" Dad muttered to Mom.

She looked a bit shamefaced, rubbing her foot. "The Internet," she admitted. "But he's very highly thought of."

"Zoob, are you ready?" said Doctor van Donkel.

"Nearly, Doctor." Several instruments were humming and little lights were blinking. Doctor Zoob was typing on a keyboard, looking intently at a little dial.

"Now," said Doctor van Donkel to Jack's mom and dad, "you must be leaving the room."

"I'd prefer to stay," said Mom.

"Of course. Excellent," said Doctor van Donkel, writing this down. "Naturally. But impossible, you know. As impossible as a flying pig, as you say, no? The instruments are very sensitive. They will be measuring psychic activity. Of course, there will be none, I am sure. I am always having hopes, but . . . no. All the same, any extra persons in the room will be confusing the readings. Too many peas spoil the porridge, as you say. Away. Away with you."

"But—," Dad protested, sounding anxious.

"No. It is impossible. Away, away." Doctor van Donkel made dangerous sweeping motions with his long arms.

Mom twisted her hands and looked like she was going to say something else. Jack could tell she wanted to stay in the study, but she wanted Doctor van Donkel to make the curse go away, and if that meant she had to leave the room . . .

After a moment, she nodded. She gave Jack an encouraging smile, and then gave Dad a look. Jack thought Dad would argue, but he didn't. Dad wanted the curse to disappear even more than Mom did. He made a sympathetic face at Jack and then turned and left the room.

"Leave it in expert hands," said Dad gruffly.

"We'll just be in the kitchen, Jack," said Mom.

Doctor van Donkel said, "Be locking the door, Zoob. There must be no interruptings."

The study was getting hotter, and Jack felt sweat trickling along his spine. The bushes outside the window seemed to be pressing up against the glass.

"Are you ready, Zoob?" asked Doctor van Donkel.

Doctor Zoob said, "Well . . ."

Jack saw he had extended a big antenna from the top of one of the instruments and was jiggling it back and forth.

"Doctor, it is very odd . . ."

"What is?"

"The readings. Very high activity. Very high. Off the scale. It must be the calibration that is wrong, I think." He typed a few things on the keyboard and jiggled with the antenna again.

"This is—," said Doctor van Donkel, and

then stopped. He was staring at something on the desk. Jack looked across too. He felt his heart lurch. There was something hairy, with lots of legs, lurking in the tangle of cables. He could see its eyes gleaming. He shrank back from the desk. Poll screeched and flew up to the top of the bookcase.

"What is happening?" said Doctor van Donkel.

"Tarantula," gasped Jack, getting to his feet and backing away toward the window. The tarantula crawled out of the wires and crouched menacingly.

There was a strange noise from outside in the garden, a high-pitched whistle. A monkey? Or some kind of bird? Jack glanced out the window, but there was nothing to see—only thick bushes, leaves, and vines. He looked back at the spider. It was motionless.

Poll gave another screech, making everyone jump.

"This is . . . ," said Doctor van Donkel. "This is . . ." He paused.

Suddenly, he gave a low, throaty laugh.

Poll shrieked. "She's coming, shipmate."

Jack's stomach did a backflip as he realized what was about to happen.

Doctor van Donkel's arms gave a few strange flaps. He started to jerk around like a puppet. He was swelling in some places and shrinking in others. His white, bony face was becoming smooth and dark. His little square beard disappeared, and his shiny bald head sprouted a thick mane of black hair. His body was twisting and writhing. It looked to Jack as if he was putting up a bit of a fight, not wanting to turn into a pirate. He was shuddering and shaking and making strange, stifled cries. For a moment, he was bald and bony again, and Jack saw a look of surprise on his face, but then he changed completely, becoming a dangerous-looking woman. Jack saw gold hoop earrings appear and tall, black leather boots with gold buckles.

She was very beautiful. She had shiny dark skin and long black hair. When she smiled, Jack saw her teeth were very even and very white. Doctor van Donkel's clothes had vanished, and the woman was wearing a full-skirted red velvet coat and a huge hat with a feather. She sat down at the desk and lounged back, crossing her feet and resting them on the desktop. She looked very relaxed, as if she had been poured into the chair, but alert, like a resting jaguar. Her belt was bristling with knives, and she had three in one hand.

Her hand gave a flick, almost too fast to see.

Jack felt a quick rush of wind and heard a *thunk*. Beside his ear a knife was stuck, quivering, in the window frame. He gulped.

"Jack Morgan," purred Tortuga Anna. "Finally, we meet. On your last day alive."

CHAPTER 10

Frightened and trapped, Jack looked desperately around the study. How could he get out of this? Tortuga Anna was watching him with a lazy smile, spinning a knife between her fingers.

Jack glanced across at the door. It was locked, of course. Jack had seen Doctor Zoob lock it and put the key in his pocket. Doctor Zoob seemed to be in a state of shock. His face was so pale it looked gray, and he was shaking like Jell-O. No help there.

Several tarantulas were climbing over the instruments and the tangle of cables on the desk. Tortuga Anna reached out an elegant hand and picked up the nearest spider. She made clicking noises to it and stroked its furry back.

Now, while she's distracted, thought Jack, and he started to edge away from the window.

Flick went Tortuga Anna's hand, and *thunk,* another knife hit the window frame, just next to Jack's shoulder. He jerked away but found that the knife had passed through the sleeve of his pajama top and pinned it to the window frame. Jack took hold of the carved bone hilt of the knife and tried to pull it out, but it was stuck firm. He jerked his arm, ripping the sleeve.

Tortuga Anna laughed, a throaty chuckle.

Poll screeched, "Tortuga Anna, we'll see the color of your insides, by the powers."

"Ah, Poll," she purred, glancing up at him. "Mayhap I'll be seeing yours."

"I'll yell, and my parents will come right away,' said Jack. "They're just outside."

Tortuga Anna gave Jack a sinister smile. She held up a knife so he could see it. The blade glinted. "I think not, Jack Morgan. Unless you have a notion to become an orphan."

Jack swallowed. Okay. No help there either. He had to deal with this himself. But what could he do? Could he try to get Doctor van Donkel back from inside Tortuga Anna, like they had with Mrs. Lemon and Hellfire Drake?

He took a steadying breath, and said, "Doctor van Donkel—"

Tortuga Anna interrupted him with a scornful laugh. "Aye, Jack Morgan. That was a pretty trick you played on my shipmate, Hellfire Drake. Mighty cunning. You have Blackstrap's brains, by the powers. But it won't work with me, by thunder." She tapped her forehead with a knife. "I've a stronger grip up here than that great hairy gorilla."

Jack believed her. He looked away.

Then he saw something that made his heart give a hopeful leap. Right away, he looked down at the floor so that Tortuga Anna wouldn't suspect what was happening. Doctor Zoob had recovered himself and was stealthily approaching her from behind. He was holding a black metal box sprouting wires. He had a brave and determined expression.

Tortuga Anna seemed to be engrossed in her spider, crooning to it. Out of the corner of his eye, Jack saw Doctor Zoob lift the hard, heavy box up over his head, and . . .

Tortuga Anna's hand, the one that wasn't holding the spider, gave a sudden flick. There was a small thud as the hilt of a knife struck Doctor Zoob on the temple, and a much louder thud as Doctor Zoob and the metal box hit the floor.

Jack gasped. "Is he . . . ?" He started toward the fallen scientist but was restrained by the knife through his sleeve.

"Dead?" said Tortuga Anna. "Nay. A headache only. I've no quarrel with him." She flicked another knife at Jack. *Thunk*. This one pinned the collar of his top to the window frame. He could feel the cold blade against his neck. "My quarrel, lad, is with you."

Flick, flick, went her hand, and *thunk, thunk,* two more knives stapled Jack's pajama top to the window frame. Each one passed so close he could feel their sharp edges touching his skin. He tried to move, but he was pinned like a bug in a museum.

"Do your worst, Tortuga Anna," screeched Poll. "Jack ain't afraid of you."

Jack gulped. He wished Poll was right, but in truth he was so frightened he thought he might throw up. He tried to think, but he was running out of ideas. Tortuga Anna was watching him, smiling, tossing a knife from hand to hand.

"One to port," she said. "One to starboard. And one right down the middle. Amidships."

Slowly, she raised the knife and curled her hand back, ready to throw.

Jack braced himself, almost hypnotized by the knife blade glinting in the long, elegant fingers. The room was very hot. There was a strange chattering noise from outside in the bushes. If only he could distract her, just for a moment.

"Mom! Dad!" he yelled, as loud as he could. "Help! Help!"

There were running feet, and then the door handle was being rattled. Tortuga Anna turned her head, and in that moment of distraction Jack flung himself forward, ripping his pajama top to shreds and freeing himself from the knives. He felt slicing pain in his side and his arm. Spinning around, he wrenched the window wide open and flung himself out into the garden.

He landed, face first, in the thick, spiny bushes beneath the window. He heard a whirring sound as a knife whizzed past his ear. Another knife almost parted his hair. He didn't stop. He rolled to his feet and forced his way blindly through the thick vegetation.

He heard a crash from behind him. The study door breaking down, he guessed. And a smash of broken glass—that must be the window. He heard Poll screech from nearby. There was a confused shouting—Mom and Dad's voices. Jack crashed blindly through the bushes. He expected to come out onto the lawn, but the thick undergrowth seemed to be everywhere. The backyard had grown into a jungle. He shoved and pushed his way through, his bare arms up to protect his face from scratches and stings. It was very hot and steamy. There were vines tangling through the bushes, trying to trip him. Big, wet leaves slapped him, and thorns tore at the remains of his pajamas. Weird-looking insects zipped past.

What else is in here? Jack wondered, on the edge of panic. *Snakes? Crocodiles?* He couldn't see more than an arm's length in any direction, just leaves and vines and strange, brightly colored flowers. Anything could be lurking.

As if to confirm this thought, there was a sudden chattering noise from somewhere to his right. Jack spun around. What was that?

He stood still and listened.

A buzzing insect. A rustle. A quiet hiss. His own breathing.

Suddenly, not very far away, a low chuckle.

A whirr, and a *thunk*. A knife with a carved whalebone hilt quivered in the mossy bark of a tree right beside him.

That was it! Jack plunged headlong into the undergrowth. Not caring about noise anymore. Just running. Vines grabbed at his ankles. Branches scratched at his face. There were strange noises. A whoop-whoop-whoop. A scream. His bare foot plunged into black, sticky mud. Panic-stricken, he yanked it out and struggled on, his feet slipping, his hands grabbing, shoving, forcing his way through the jungle.

He heard a screech from somewhere overhead. Poll. He could hear voices calling. Mom and Dad? He crashed and bashed his way through, fighting for breath.

He emerged into a small sunlit clearing on the edge of a deep pool. One more step, and he would have plunged in. Jack bent double, panting for breath, drenched in sweat, covered in scratches and mud.

Poll suddenly flew down and landed on his head.

"Shipmate," he said. "She's—" But before he could continue, Tortuga Anna stalked out of the jungle to stand at the other side of the clearing.

She looked as if she had just been for a stroll in the park. Her clothes were immaculate, even her tall black boots were still shiny. She had a tarantula on her shoulder and two or three knives in each hand.

She smiled ferociously. "Jack Morgan," she said. "By the powers, you won't slip your cable again, or I'm mistook."

She started to pace around the mossy edge of the pool toward Jack and Poll.

"Do your worst, Tortuga Anna," shrieked Poll. Not for the first time, Jack wished Poll would shut up. He started to edge around the pool, away from the pirate.

There was a whirr, a thud, and a knife stuck into the moss just in front of his bare foot.

"Avast, lad," said Tortuga Anna. "Hold fast."

Jack stopped and turned toward her. She was coming closer, smiling, looking deadly. Jack was helpless. He was wearing only his pajamas, which were ripped and ragged. He was covered in mud and scratches and moss. He was exhausted and frightened. What could he do?

Tortuga Anna drew closer.

Desperately, Jack stared at her, weighing his options. If he turned to run, she would fling a knife at him, and she wouldn't miss. If he stayed where he was, then it'd be even easier for her. How could he save himself?

Suddenly there was a rustling and angry muttering from the thick jungle on the far side of the pool, and Dad pushed his way into the clearing. He looked muddy and scratched and furious in his pajamas and his black lace-up shoes.

"Hey, you!" he shouted. "Leave Jack alone!"

Tortuga Anna turned her head.

All at once, a line of writing appeared in Jack's head, as if by magic. *"Strangely enough, most pirates could not swim."* Where had he seen that? He didn't stop to think.

Tortuga Anna's head was turned toward Dad. She was ready to throw a knife at him. At Dad. Jack had to do something, fast.

He dived at her and grabbed her around the waist. For a moment, they struggled together, teetering on the edge of the pool. Jack could tell he wouldn't be able to hold on to her for very long; she was too strong.

He could feel the knives in her belt pricking against his chest. Then she was wrenching him off. Jack struggled. He shoved. He tried to get a grip on her again but, with a laugh, she flung him away. He landed with a thump on the mossy ground, panting for breath.

She turned away lazily. Jack could see Dad hurrying around the pool toward her. Slowly, she pulled out a knife and stood poised, ready to throw.

With an angry yell, Jack launched himself again. This time, he grabbed her legs. She kicked out at him, but he hung on. He pushed with all his strength. His feet were slipping on the moss. He shoved again, as hard as he could.

All at once, she slipped and lost her balance. She gave an angry cry, and they fell together into the pool with a huge splash.

Jack felt the cold water close over his head. He kicked out and came to the surface.

Treading water, he looked around, gasping for breath. There was no sign of Tortuga Anna. Poll was flying in circles above the water, screeching with excitement. Dad was kicking off his shoes, scanning the water, ready to dive in.

Was she gone? If she couldn't swim, then surely she would have to disappear when she fell in the water. Then Doctor van Donkel would be able to return. But where was he?

Jack had a sudden frightening thought. What if Doctor van Donkel couldn't swim either? He took a deep breath and dived down to the bottom of the pool. Oddly, his outstretched fingers felt smooth tiles. Part of his brain thought, *Of course. This is our own pool. In the backyard.*

He came up for breath then dived again. This time, he saw a dark shape.

He surfaced for another breath and saw Dad standing on the edge, ready to dive.

"Down there," gasped Jack.

Together, they dived down and brought Doctor van Donkel to the surface. He was heavy, waterlogged, and bony. He started spluttering and gasping and spitting out water.

They swam him to the edge and Dad hauled him out. They laid him down in the sunshine.

He looked confused and very wet. His white coat was soaked through.

"What happened?" he asked dazedly, gasping for air.

"The curse happened," said Jack.

CHAPTER 11

Doctor van Donkel and Doctor Zoob stayed for breakfast. Doctor van Donkel was dressed in some of Dad's clothes, which were a bit short for him, and he was showing a lot of ankle and wrist. He still seemed a bit confused, but he was excited by the experience. He said he had a vague memory of turning into Tortuga Anna, and the next thing he could remember was waking up in the pool, being dragged to the side by Jack and Dad.

"There's a paper in this," he said, writing frantically. "A lecture tour. What an experience I am having. The name van Donkel will be famous!" He turned a page of his pad and buttered a piece of toast, humming what sounded like a sea shanty. He flipped the butter knife into the air. It spun across the table and landed neatly, point first, in the margarine.

Doctor Zoob had a big bruise on his forehead where Tortuga Anna had knocked him out with the hilt of her knife. He kept saying, "Never seen anything like that," to himself, and giggling in a manic sort of way. The two doctors ate lots of toast and drank lots of coffee, and then Dad went off to call a taxi to take them to their hotel.

Jack watched them drive away.

Back in the kitchen, Poll was finishing up the toast. For a small bird, he had a huge appetite. He waved a piece of toast at Jack. "Jack, lad. That's two battles in two days. A prodigious effort."

Jack sank down into a kitchen chair. He hurt all over, from scratches and bruises and exhaustion. There were some long scratches on his side and on his arm from Tortuga Anna's knives. Mom had put some ointment on them, but they still stung.

"Ha ha ha, Tortuga Anna'll be fearful angry," predicted Poll. "And how about that?" His beady eye looked across at Dad. "Hey, you! Leave Jack alone!" he mimicked.

Dad tried to look modest. "I just didn't think," he said, proudly. "I just saw Jack there, in danger . . ."

"A mighty challenge," said Poll.

Dad squared his shoulders. "Well, I don't know . . . It was nothing, really," he said, looking very pleased with himself. He made a thrust in the air with his spoon, and muttered threateningly, "Get back, you sea scum!"

Mom chimed in. "Yes, well, that's all very fine. But look at the state of you. And look at the garden. It's still a jungle. There are *things* in there."

To confirm this, there came a whoop-whoop-whoop noise from the backyard.

"What's that, for heaven's sake?" asked Mom. "Really. I think this curse thing has gone too far. Jack, you go back to your room and lock yourself in. Look what happened when you came out today. I want you to be safe."

Jack groaned at the thought of returning to his empty bedroom.

"I mean it, Jack," said Mom firmly.

Before Jack could argue, there was a knock at the front door. Jack got up to answer it, but Mom snapped, "No, stay there," and went herself.

She came back with Rachel.

"Just a minute or two," Mom said, "because

Jack's going back into his room, right away."

Jack's "No, I'm not," was drowned out by Poll's screech of "Shipmate!" and Rachel saying, "Hello, Jack. Hello, Poll. Hello, Mr. Jones," as she sat down at the table. "What's been happening here? Have you seen your backyard? It's like a jungle or something. And there are noises in there. Weird noises. What's in there? Monkeys, maybe. What happened to you, Jack? Wow, where'd you get those scratches? What's been going on? You've been in another fight, haven't you?"

Between them, they explained the events of the morning so far. Rachel gasped and exclaimed. Finally, she said admiringly, "Wow, Mr. Jones. 'Hey, you! Leave Jack alone!' I wish I'd been here."

"A mighty battle," confirmed Poll.

"So who's next, Poll?" asked Rachel with interest, picking up toast crumbs with the tips of her fingers. "Captain Kelso?"

"Shipmate, don't even think of it," whispered Poll, glancing over his shoulder nervously. "Mayhap, he won't come at all. You don't want to be meeting him, that monstrous, bloodthirsty man."

Jack shivered. He remembered the little picture of Captain Kelso in *All About Pirates*. The gaunt face with the dark, dead eyes. The evil smile, showing the pointed teeth.

Mom, who had been standing anxiously at the door, clapped her hands together and said, "That's enough. Come on, Jack. Up to your room."

Jack could tell she really meant it. Reluctantly, he got to his feet.

Suddenly, Rachel said, "What's that smell?"

Everyone sniffed.

"Burnt toast?" said Dad uncertainly.

From the backyard came a sharp scream.

"What was that?" said Jack.

It was already hot in the kitchen, but suddenly it seemed very close and intense. Jack looked around the room. Everyone was jumpy and alert, glances shooting here and there. Poll cocked his head to one side.

"Something's burning," said Mom jerkily.

"And something's moving," gasped Rachel, jumping to her feet and pointing a shaking finger at the kitchen counter, where there was a pile of crumpled papers. As they all watched, there was a movement underneath. Several hairy legs appeared.

Poll gave a screech of excitement, flew up, and landed on Jack's head. "They're coming back, shipmate," he shrieked.

"But—," said Jack. *Not now, it's too soon,* he thought. *I'm exhausted. Not now.*

"Jack, quickly," said Mom desperately, grabbing him by the arm and dragging him toward the door. "There might be time to—"

She stopped talking, gave a gasp, and let go.

"There might—," she started to say. Jack backed away, horrified. It had been bad enough to see Mrs. Lemon and then Doctor van Donkel turn into pirates. But it was sickening to see it happen to Mom.

She started to jerk about, her arms flapping. She seemed to be trying to say something to him, but all that was coming out were stifled bits of words that he couldn't understand. She was growing taller. Her short brown hair was growing longer and becoming a shiny black. Her skin was getting darker.

"Mom," yelled Jack. "Mom, no!"

"Jack!" gasped Rachel.

He tore his gaze away from Mom for just a second. Rachel was staring, horror-struck, at Jack's dad.

Jack looked.

Dad was gone.

Instead, looming at the end of the table, was a hairy giant. His thick red beard was sparking and smoking. Dad's pajama pants were stretched to bursting over his huge belly. He was holding an enormous cutlass. He brought it down on the kitchen table with a crash, and the table cracked down the middle. He laughed loudly.

It was Hellfire Drake.

Poll screeched again and again, flapping his wings.

Jack backed away into a corner of the kitchen. At one end of the table, where Dad had been, Hellfire Drake was roaring and laughing and waving his sword around menacingly. At the other end, where Mom had been, was Tortuga Anna. She was looking deadly, flipping a little knife in one hand, a tarantula on her shoulder. She gave a throaty chuckle.

Jack tried to swallow over the lump in his throat.

"Arrr," roared Hellfire Drake. "Blackstrap's brat." He slashed his sword down onto one of the kitchen chairs, and then crushed the dismembered parts under his huge boots.

"Jack Morgan," purred Tortuga Anna. She flicked a knife at him. *Whirr. Thunk.* It quivered in the countertop, a millimeter from his hand.

Jack glanced at Rachel. She looked terrified.

"Do your worst," shrieked Poll to the pirates. "Jack ain't afraid of you."

Jack felt his heart sink. Would he really have to spend his whole life running away from these two maniacs?

"Run, Jack Morgan," offered Tortuga Anna, as if she'd read his mind. She took two steps away from the kitchen door. "Make your escape."

Jack looked across at the door. He could run up to his bedroom. He could run into the backyard and hide in the jungle.

Whirr, thunk. Another knife. Jack felt the rush of air as it whizzed past. It struck a cupboard door, right next to his ear.

"Run, lad, or fight here," said Tortuga Anna, with a touch of impatience.

"Come on, shipmate," screeched Poll excitedly. Jack could feel him hopping up and down, ready to go. He flew off Jack's head and started circling the room, screaming and shrieking.

"Arrgh," roared Hellfire Drake. "Blackstrap's brat. Run, run, run like a rabbit." He raised his sword up above his head and brought it swishing down. Jack jerked sideways, and the sword cut into the counter, embedding itself into the laminate.

No, thought Jack. He couldn't spend his life running away. And he couldn't fight Mom and Dad. They were still here, somewhere inside these homicidal pirates.

He'd had enough.

He took a breath, looking from one to the other. He knew what he had to do, what he had to say. This was it.

"No," he said.

CHAPTER 12

Hellfire Drake roared in anger. It was deafening. Jack flinched.

The huge pirate lifted his sword high above his head. Jack didn't move, despite the sick feeling in his stomach and the weak, shaking feeling in his legs. He stood still, biting his bottom lip, looking up at the shiny curved blade.

"Run, Blackstrap's brat," Hellfire Drake thundered.

Jack didn't move.

"Jack," said Rachel urgently.

"Shipmate," screeched Poll.

Jack shook his head. This was it.

With a swish, Hellfire Drake brought the sword down. Rachel screamed. Poll shrieked. Jack shut his eyes.

Nothing.

Jack opened his eyes and saw that Hellfire Drake's cold steel blade had stopped barely a fraction of an inch from his head. It was so close he could feel the sharp edge touching his hair. There was a silence. No one moved or even breathed. Then Hellfire Drake lifted the sword up again and gave a crack of thunderous laughter.

"Ha ha ha ha," he roared. "Blackstrap's brat. He's got Blackstrap's guts, by thunder!"

"I knew it," said Jack, feeling light-headed with relief. "I just knew it. You're not trying to kill me at all, are you?"

"Blackstrap's guts and Blackstrap's brains," remarked Tortuga Anna, sinking into a chair at the end of the table, stretching out her long legs and stroking her spider. She flipped the knife in her hand into the air and it landed, point first, in the tabletop. "He has the look of Blackstrap about him, by the powers. But for the gold tooth and the hook, of course."

Poll landed on Jack's head.

Hellfire Drake poked his curved sword into his belt and sat down, turning the chair around backward and resting his huge tree-trunk arms on its back.

"Well, Jack Morgan . . . ," said Tortuga Anna.

"Jack Jones," said Jack in exasperation. "Jack

Jones. There's no such person as Jack Morgan."

Rachel sat down, looking pale. "What's going on?" she asked.

"This curse. It's not about killing me at all, is it?" said Jack, looking from one pirate to the other. "It's about frightening me. It's about chasing me around and around and driving me nuts. Isn't it? It's about ruining my life."

"Well, lad . . . ," said Tortuga Anna.

"I thought so," said Jack scornfully. "I mean, if you'd wanted to, you could have chopped me up in one second instead of chasing me around the classroom like that," he said to Hellfire Drake. "And you could have chucked a knife *into* me, instead of all around the edges," he said to Tortuga Anna. "Huh! After all, Great-Uncle Mungo was cursed too. And how old was he when he died?"

"Ninety-three," admitted Tortuga Anna, inspecting her fingernails and looking a bit ashamed.

"Yes, well," snapped Jack. "And I bet he spent most of his time running away from you two. Never seeing his family. Never seeing anyone he cared about. Well, you're not doing that to me. You're not going to wreck my life. I've had enough. My teacher hates me, the classroom is smashed to pieces. Our whole class has detention forever. My bedroom's empty, the backyard's a jungle. I'm covered with scratches, my arm hurts, my head hurts, my feet hurt. Now you've wrecked the kitchen table. Well done. But it ends here. There's no point going on, now that I know what you're up to. You can't frighten me anymore. That's it. You can give me my mom and dad back, too." Jack stopped for breath.

"It's not as easy as that, lad," said Tortuga Anna. "A curse is no light thing. And this is a mighty powerful one. Blackstrap betrayed us, lad. He betrayed the accord."

"Look," said Jack, a bit more calmly. "I'm sorry about what Blackstrap Morgan did to you. Poll told me the story. That's terrible. He did a terrible thing. I'm really sorry about that." Jack looked back and forth between Hellfire Drake and Tortuga Anna. They didn't say anything. "Really, really sorry," he went on. "But it wasn't my fault. I wasn't there."

The two pirates exchanged a look.

"Well, I can try to make it up to you. Wait

here," said Jack. He put Poll down on the kitchen counter and went upstairs. In the hallway outside his bedroom he found the wooden box containing Great-Uncle Mungo's presents. He took it down to the kitchen, sat down at the table, and opened it up.

Carefully, he lifted the precious things out and laid them on the cracked tabletop. The gold cigarette lighter. The sparkly buckles. The sharp little knife. The coins from all over the world. He piled the coins neatly into gleaming stacks.

They watched him in silence.

"There," he said. "It's not the treasure that Blackstrap stole from you, nothing like it, I guess. But these are the best things I've got. Uncle Mungo gave them to me. I'd like you to have them. In return for my mom and dad."

There was a silence.

Suddenly, Hellfire Drake gave a huge sniff. It sounded like a drain being cleared. "Mighty thoughtful of you, Jack, lad," he said, in a voice that sounded like he was about to burst into tears. He pulled a handkerchief out of his pocket and blew his nose loudly.

"Look," Jack said, picking up the cigarette lighter and flicking the little wheel. It ignited with a bright yellow flame.

Hellfire Drake's eyes lit up in response. "Shiver me timbers."

"You take that," said Jack, handing it to him. "You can use it, you know, to light your . . . well, whatever it is that makes your beard burn like that."

"Slow fuses, lad," said Hellfire Drake. "And it's monstrous difficult, with flint, to get a light. That'll be mighty handy. Thank ye."

He took the little lighter in his huge, hairy hand and flicked the wheel. He smiled in delight to see the little flame pop up.

Jack turned to Tortuga Anna. He held out the knife. "You take this," he said. "I think you'll like it. It's very sharp. And take these too." He handed her the sparkly buckles. "For your boots or, I don't know, whatever."

Tortuga Anna tested the edge of the knife and balanced it experimentally on one finger. Then she turned over the buckles in her elegant hands. The sparkly stones caught the light and flashed. Jack couldn't tell what she was thinking.

"And take all these," Jack said. "For the rest of the crew." He shuffled the piles of coins toward her. "They're probably not worth much, but they're nice."

She picked up the coins and looked at Jack. "Well, Jack," she said. "Like Hellfire says, this is mighty thoughtful." She stopped.

"It's fair," said Jack. "Blackstrap stole your treasure . . ."

"Well," said Tortuga Anna. She seemed lost in thought. Then her eyes sparkled. "Well, lad, I won't be abandoning the Curse, and that's the truth of it. A prodigious curse. And I won't say I haven't had the joy of it, chasing all Blackstrap's descendants to hell and back. But, Jack, you have reason on your side. And you have a look of Blackstrap about you . . ."

There was a silence for a few minutes. Then Jack said, "So, can I have my mom and dad back?"

She nodded. "Aye, Jack. We'll go. Back to Skeleton Island. For now."

"Aha!" screeched Poll. "You're on the run now, you bilge rats—"

"Shut up, Poll," snapped Jack. "Just shut your beak, you . . . you . . ."

Tortuga Anna laughed. "Poll, shiver my timbers if you don't find yourself roasted and served up for Sunday dinner one of these days. Although you'd be tough on the teeth and no mistake. Listen, Jack, lad. Before we go. Two things. One is this." She flipped one of her knives out of her belt and tossed it up into the air. It spun and pierced the table in front of Jack, point down, quivering. "For that box of yours," she said, nodding toward the empty box. Jack looked at the knife. It had a bone hilt, carved with a skull and crossbones. Cautiously, he reached over and pulled the knife out of the table.

"For me?" he asked, running his fingers over the smooth carving.

She nodded and said casually, "You do have the look of Blackstrap about you, lad. I always thought him a good man. Even now, it's hard to believe . . ." She stopped and shook her head sadly. Then she gave a sigh and went on more firmly. "And the other thing, Jack, is this: Captain Kelso will be mighty angry. You'll have to keep a weather eye out for him, lad. What you say about Hellfire and myself, it's the truth. We're in it for the cruise. For the adventure. For the joy of it, if you like. With him, it's life or death on a lee shore, and make no mistake. He's a dangerous, vicious man." She gave a shudder. "So set a watch for him. And take care, lad."

Hellfire Drake gave another enormous snort into his handkerchief. "That's the lay of it, Jack," he said. "And here, shipmate." He reached into a pocket of his trousers, fumbled around for a moment, brought out another snotty handkerchief, a shark's tooth, a bundle of little firecrackers, something that looked like a shrunken head, a tiny knitted teddy bear, and, finally, a coin, which he tossed to Jack. "A doubloon," he said. "Pirate treasure, lad."

Jack caught the coin. It was unexpectedly heavy. It had an uneven edge and a rich sheen. He turned it over and over in his hand.

He looked up at Hellfire Drake, intending to thank him, but he was already changing back into Dad, shrinking down as if someone was letting the air out of him. Jack glanced down to the other end of the table, but Tortuga Anna was also changing back.

"Wait . . . ," said Jack. He wanted to say something. Sorry. Thank you. Good-bye.

But they were gone.

There was a smoky smell in the air, a cracked table, and two dazed and confused parents who looked like they were just waking up from very disturbing dreams.

CHAPTER 13

Jack went to the door to see Rachel off to school. He couldn't believe it was still only morning.

"Why don't you come, Jack?" Rachel said. "Mrs. Lemon's really different. All that singing and dancing. It's amazing."

"That'll wear off, Poll says," said Jack, watching a small red and blue bird zip out from the jungle behind the house and zoom across the front yard.

"Well then, come and see her before she's back to normal. By Monday, she'll be all 'Rachel Marconi. What are you wearing?' again, and 'Kindly write out the school rules a hundred times. In your best handwriting.' You know. Anyway, you're safe from the curse now. Except for . . ."

"All the same," said Jack quickly, before Rachel could say "Captain Kelso." Just the sound of the name gave him chills. "Mom says I can stay home."

"Hmm. I heard her. With a yo ho ho, and all," said Rachel.

Jack giggled. Once they'd gotten over their disorientation, Jack had told them that Hellfire Drake and Tortuga Anna would not be coming back. He hadn't mentioned Captain Kelso. Jack didn't want to think about him at all. Mom and Dad had been happy to hear the news that Jack was safe, and they had started singing sea shanties. They were still going. He could hear their cheerful voices mingled with Poll's loud raspy singing coming from the kitchen.

"Well, if you won't, you won't." Rachel put on her backpack. "Can't blame you. Have a nice rest. Bye."

"See you," said Jack. He waved and went back into the house.

A peacock feather in my hat,
And a cutlass in my hand,
I'll sail the sea, a pirate free,
And never live on land.

Jack stood in the doorway of the kitchen, watching. Poll was singing very, very loudly, like a blast siren, with his eyes shut, hopping from foot to foot. Mom was conducting enthusiastically with a butter knife. Dad was rocking back and forth, banging his hand on the table, roaring out the chorus.

Shipmates all, through storm and squall,
Across the briny sea,
Rant and roar and treasure galore,
A pirate's life for me.

Jack wondered how long this would take to wear off.

Mom spotted him standing in the doorway and gave him a wave. "Jack, shipmate," she said. "There you are. Come and join in."

It was weird hearing her call him "shipmate," but she was looking happier than she had for days.

Dad gave Jack a wave, but he didn't stop singing and rocking in his chair. Jack couldn't remember the last time he'd heard Dad sing.

He giggled again. It was so weird, it was funny. He shook his head at Mom, waved at Dad, and went upstairs. His bed was still propped up in the hallway outside his room. He pulled the mattress off and dragged it into his bedroom. He went back for the pillow, but he didn't bother with the bed coverings. It was too hot, anyway. He was exhausted. He felt tired all the way through, right to his bones. He flopped down on the mattress and closed his eyes.

The room was very hot; the air was thick and still. A fly buzzed against the window. The singing from downstairs went on and on, accompanied by thumping and banging. It sounded like they had started dancing. Jack could have shut the door, but he didn't. The noise didn't bother him at all.

When Jack woke up it was dark outside. Was it evening already? It didn't feel that late. He got up and looked out the window. There were huge purply-black thunderclouds piled up in the sky. It was even hotter than before, steamy and oppressive.

Jack felt sweaty and sticky, so he took a

shower and then found a clean T-shirt and pair of shorts. He looked at the torn and filthy pajamas—he'd need new ones for sure now.

It was so dark outside that the lights were on in the kitchen. Mom was cooking. She smiled. "Ready for lunch, darling?"

"Shipmate!" screeched Poll welcomingly. He was perched on the back of a chair, eating a piece of pineapple.

Jack looked around. "What's all this?"

"Breadfruit," said Mom, pointing with a wooden spoon. "Plantains, pineapples, coconut, molasses."

"Where'd it all come from?" asked Jack, bemused. He'd never seen breadfruit, which were green and round, or plantains, which were like big bananas.

"From the supermarket," said Mom. "I went down to get something for lunch, and there was this new section. Sacks of rice and beans, boxes of spices. We're having spicy coconut fish, johnnycake, and plantains for lunch."

Jack wondered if the supermarket owners realized they'd been cursed by pirates. The food smelled spicy and exotic. When Mom filled the plates, Jack carried them to the dining room table.

Dad came in, covered with bits of jungle. He had leaves in his hair and his clothes were stained with moss and mud. He slapped his hands together, his face bright and happy and dripping with sweat. "There you are, Jack," he shouted. "Excellent. How are you feeling? Better? You can come out with me after lunch— I've been clearing a path to the pool, ha ha."

Lunch was delicious. Everyone ate a lot, despite the stifling heat. Jack licked the last dribble of delicious sauce off his knife. Normally, this would have made Mom or Dad say something about his table manners, but today they didn't even notice.

"A prodigious meal," said Poll appreciatively, bowing to Mom and burping loudly. "Mighty toothsome."

Dad leaned back and scratched his stomach. "Arr," he said. "You're right there, Poll."

Jack giggled. Dad was still sounding like Hellfire Drake.

"Well, come on, lad," said Dad, getting to his feet, stretching and burping even louder than

Poll. "There's a storm coming, or I'm mistook. I want to get this path widened before the weather changes."

"Aye, off you go," said Mom. "I'll clean up here." She flipped the serving spoon into the air. It spun across the table and landed neatly in the dish that had held the plaintains. "Make everything shipshape."

Jack, with Poll riding on his head, followed Dad outside. The thick jungle filled the backyard, creeping up the walls of the house. Jack looked up at the sky. The clouds were piling up like mashed potatoes, if mashed potatoes could be a dark, ominous purple. The air felt thick and humid.

"Come on, Jack," said Dad. He marched off into the jungle in the direction of the pool. Jack could see he had already cleared a bit of a path. There were thick walls of leaves and ferns and vines on both sides and overhead, so it was like walking along a narrow green corridor.

Jack followed Dad along the path to the pool. There was a huge pile of leaves and vines and branches in the clearing, already as high as Jack's head.

"When we're done, we'll have a bonfire," said Dad. "A feast, maybe. Singing and dancing, ha ha. We'll have the Marconis over."

Poll screeched and Jack could feel him hopping up and down with excitement.

"Now," said Dad, brandishing the garden shears enthusiastically. "I'm going to widen the path. How about you bring the stuff back here and pile it up?"

Jack nodded. "Okay."

Dad went back down the path and started chopping into the jungle with his shears. Jack collected the leaves and branches, dragged them back to the clearing, and heaved them up on top of the huge pile.

For a while, they worked in silence. To start with, Poll had encouraged Jack by shouting "One, Two, One, Two," like Mr. Stockton. Jack had explained to him that if he didn't stop, he would be turned into Sunday dinner, like Tortuga Anna had suggested. Poll had sulked silently for a while, before launching into an encouraging shanty. Jack told him to shut his beak. Poll gave an offended cluck and flew off. Jack suspected he had gone back inside to finish the remains of lunch.

Today it was good working with Dad. Usually Dad was so particular that Jack felt like he couldn't do anything right. But Dad with just a touch of Hellfire Drake in him was much easier to get along with. He was humming happily to himself and giving Jack cheerful grins over his shoulder as he hacked away at the thick vegetation, throwing great piles of it out onto the path.

The day got steadily darker. From the clearing, Jack could see the clouds getting even thicker. Lightning flashes lit up their undersides. The tops of the jungle trees were starting to wave about in the strengthening wind. There were a few drops of rain.

Jack went along to where Dad was cutting and slashing at the jungle in the shelter of the pathway, and told him about the weather. Thunder rumbled.

"Okay, then," Dad said, straightening up and stretching his back. "I'll just go get the tools and things we left in the clearing. You follow with the rest of this, and we'll finish up for now. Good work, Jack. Thanks for your help."

Dad collected a big armful of vines and leaves and a couple of big branches and disappeared around a bend in the path toward the pool. Jack started to pick up the last pieces of jungle that Dad had chopped off. He straightened up, his arms full, and took two steps down the path.

Just then, the rain really started.

It was like someone had opened a door in the sky and emptied a lake through it. Within one second, Jack was soaked to the skin and gasping for breath. It was like being underwater. He could barely see the path. The tremendous hammering noise of the rain was even louder than the cracks of thunder. He stumbled a few steps toward the pool, then realized it would be smarter to go back to the house. He dropped the branches and leaves he had been carrying, turned around as well as he could, and started back, arms outstretched.

He stumbled along, half running, eyes shut, hands groping through the almost solid wall of water. His hair was plastered flat onto his head, water streaming down his face.

Crash! He stumbled into a thick, thorny

bush. He jerked back and started forward again. Something grabbed him around the ankle. *Splat!* He fell full-length. He reached down, felt for the thick vine, and pulled his foot clear. He scrambled to his feet and plunged straight into a bush with large, flat leaves that clung to him wetly. He pulled himself free and tried to get back onto the path.

The rain was as heavy as ever, hammering down. Jack blundered on, sometimes on the path, sometimes not. He thought Dad would catch up with him and help him back to the house. Or Mom would come out and get him. Or Poll would appear. But they didn't.

On and on. Surely he should be back at the house by now? His outstretched hands kept expecting to feel the back door. His feet should soon trip over the back step. Surely he had already gone too far? He must have gone the wrong way somehow.

At last, the rain seemed to be letting up. Jack could see his way through the falling raindrops a bit better. In front, the path curved around and came out into a clearing. It was brighter up ahead. He must have turned himself around, he thought, and headed back toward the pool.

He stumbled forward, around the curve, and out into the clearing. He looked around, just as the rain stopped altogether.

He was standing at the edge of the jungle. A turquoise blue sea was lapping at the edge of a white sandy beach.

It was completely strange and completely deserted.

CHAPTER 14

Jack stared blankly down the white sand to the lapping sea. At the curving beach with the fringe of jungle. What was happening? Where was he?

"Poll?" he called.

There was no answer. He looked up into the empty blue sky. No small green parrot flew down, screeching. Nothing.

"Dad?" Jack shouted. "Hello? Anyone?"

Nothing.

It felt weird, here. Not just because he was unexpectedly on a tropical beach, a long way from home. Of course, that was seriously weird. It was as if he were in a dream, as if things were not exactly real, and he might wake up any minute and find himself back in his bedroom. Jack reached out and touched the trunk of a palm tree. It felt solid and slightly rough. It felt real. What did they say about dreams? Pinch yourself to wake up. Jack pinched himself hard on the leg. It hurt a bit, but nothing happened.

He looked up and down the beach. The sunshine sparkled on the sea, the palm trees waved gently. A line of surf broke on a reef and three or four white birds flew past.

Well, thought Jack, trying to be sensible, trying to think. *One minute, backyard; next minute, strange beach. Okay.* He could deal with this. He should be used to weird things happening by now. The best thing to do, obviously, was to retrace his steps. Maybe his whole house had been transported to the beach. Then he'd find himself back home right away.

This was a cheerful thought, and he turned and started back. The thick, stifling jungle closed in around him. Mossy tree trunks, big flat leaves, creepers, and ferns formed walls at the sides of the path. Tangled vines looped down from the canopy. The path was sand and mossy earth, with big gnarled tree roots winding their way across. Jack walked carefully and quietly. The thick jungle made him feel uneasy. Anything could be hiding in the shadows. He felt invisible eyes watching him. His skin prickled.

The only noises were the sound of the sea, which was growing fainter, and a constant hum of insects. After a few minutes, the narrow, winding path started to slope uphill, curving around mossy rocks and overhanging branches.

Suddenly, Jack heard footsteps behind him. He spun around, but there was no one to be seen.

"Hello? Who's there?" he called, trying to keep his voice steady.

There was no answer. He took a couple of cautious steps back down the path. It was deserted.

He heard a sudden whispering noise behind him. He looked back quickly. Nothing. It must have been the wind, he told himself nervously. As quietly as he could, listening all the time, he continued up the path. Soon it was climbing steeply. Sometimes there were handy branches that he could grab to help pull himself up. Up and up.

Once, the path crossed a rickety wooden bridge near a little waterfall. Jack stopped and, leaning precariously, poked his hot, sweaty head underneath the cool trickling water. It felt excellent. He took off his T-shirt, wet it in the waterfall, and put it back on. He drank a couple of mouthfuls of water, ignoring Dad's voice in his head, which was talking about germs and microbes. Feeling refreshed, he went on up the path.

Further on, he heard the whispering again. He had stopped for a short rest, and it came from behind him, sudden and very close. Jack spun around. There was nothing, just a thick wall of jungle. Determinedly, he fought down his rising panic. Probably just the noise of the wind, he said to himself again. Or maybe a little animal. He didn't really believe it, but he tried to.

The path wasn't taking him home. But, he thought, it must go somewhere. Jack kept climbing. It became so steep that sometimes he had to cling on with just his fingers and toes, grab the top of the rock, and haul himself over. Grab, heave, scrape, up and up.

And suddenly, he was at the top. Panting and sweating, his legs shaking from the climb, Jack found himself out in the sunshine.

Shading his eyes, he turned and looked at the view.

He felt a jolt of shock.

He was on an island.

He had come out from the jungle onto a high headland. There were small, scrubby bushes, big rocks here and there, and sand. From up here he could see the whole island curving away below him. There were two white beaches, jungle, a far line of surf at the edge of the lagoon, and a shoal of smaller islands strung out from the far end of the big one, like baby ducks following their mother.

Carefully, Jack scanned the horizon. It was a straight line, all the way around, dividing the sea from the sky. As perfect as if it had been drawn in Mrs. Lemon's geometry class. It was empty. No other land. No ships or planes. Nothing but sea and sky.

Jack was overwhelmed by a sense of hopelessness. How would he ever get home? He remembered reading about pirates being left on deserted islands in *All About Pirates*. Marooning, it was called. Had he been marooned? Left here forever? But . . .

At that moment, he heard a sound. It was a slight dry cough. He slowly turned around.

A figure was standing there. With a chill of fear, Jack recognized him right away. It was Captain Kelso.

He was dressed in black. He had a black hat, which he wore sideways, a black coat with shiny silver buttons, and high black boots. He was holding a long, narrow sword. But the thing that Jack noticed most about him was his face. It was thin and gaunt. His skin was a dead gray, a darker gray around his deep-set eyes. Captain Kelso had no color at all. He seemed to be almost transparent. He looked like an old black-and-white photo, or a ghost.

"Jack Morgan," he said, in a voice like a cold wind. "Blackstrap's spawn."

Jack wanted to say, *No. Not Jack Morgan, Jack Jones,* but the words died before they left his mouth. He shivered.

"You have the look of him," said Captain Kelso, stepping closer. He bared his teeth. Jack saw they were pointed, like a shark's. Captain Kelso whipped his sword through the air with a hissing noise. "I despised him," he said. "I should have ended this long ago. But I will end it now. Here, on Skeleton Island, where it started."

Jack wondered distantly how he had ever been frightened of Hellfire Drake or Tortuga Anna. They'd just been having fun—scary, maniac fun, maybe—but this was deadly serious.

Captain Kelso took two menacing steps toward Jack. Suddenly, there was the whispering noise again. Jack saw some faint transparent shapes moving behind Captain Kelso. Like the shimmers in the air on a hot day. Captain Kelso turned his head toward the sound, and Jack seized his chance and ran.

He zigzagged around the rocks, swerving and ducking, skidding on the sand. If he could get off the headland, maybe he could hide in the jungle. But he had to get away from Captain Kelso first. He dived behind a big rock and flattened himself against it. He froze still and tried not to breathe.

There was silence, but for the distant surf. Then Jack heard a soft footfall. He edged carefully, silently, away from the noise, keeping his back to the rock. Listening.

Nothing.

A small noise, as a pebble was dislodged. Jack held his breath.

Nothing.

Jack edged a little further along the rock. He craned around and saw Captain Kelso an arm's length away. He was standing still, sword ready, listening. Jack shrank back. He must have made some kind of noise, because Captain Kelso whipped around, sickeningly fast. Without a pause, Jack shot out of his hiding place and sprinted as fast as he could. Ducking and weaving and zigzagging. Skidding and slipping. He could hear footsteps close behind and the zing of Captain Kelso's sword blade striking rock.

As he ran, Jack was half aware of the whispering noises again. Louder now. A confused jumble of words, coming and going like the wind. He heard Captain Kelso's footsteps pause, as if the whispering noises were distracting him.

Jack swerved around a rock and, suddenly, the ground seemed to give way beneath him. He plunged through some stunted bushes and into a shallow pit. He lay on the sand, winded.

The whispering was all around now, making it hard to hear anything else. Jack expected to see Captain Kelso's evil face appear over the edge of the pit. He tried to get a solid footing, but the ground was too crumbly and soft. He finally got one foot on something hard and levered himself cautiously up to see over the tops of the little bushes.

Captain Kelso was just a few yards away. At first, it looked to Jack like he was swatting flies with his sword. He was spinning around angrily, jabbing away at the empty air. The whispering was growing louder. Then Jack could see a shimmering disturbance in the air, and he realized that Captain Kelso was fighting something invisible.

Jack ducked down again and tried to decide what to do. He looked down at the sandy floor of the pit and felt his stomach turn over. The solid thing that he had been standing on was a skull. A human skull. He shrank away from it in horror. It stared at him out of the sand, two gaping eyeholes and a row of grinning teeth. One gold tooth glinted in the sunshine. There was a round hole in the front of the skull. It looked like a bullet hole.

Jack felt something sharp digging into his leg. He scrabbled around in the sand and unearthed a metal hook and some dry white bones. He held up the hook in front of his face. Somehow it seemed significant. Important. But what . . . ?

Suddenly, Jack saw. And then he understood.

He felt anger start to burn inside him. He picked up the skull in one hand, the hook in the other. These were the remains of Blackstrap Morgan. Blackstrap had a hook and a gold tooth, Jack knew. And here was his skeleton, with a bullet hole in the skull. On the headland of Skeleton Island, where the treasure had been buried. He hadn't stolen the treasure and escaped in a small boat, like Poll had said. He'd been murdered.

Suddenly, Captain Kelso's face appeared over the edge of the shallow pit. He looked menacingly down at Jack. His face went a paler gray at the sight of the skull and the hook. The whispering was all around; it was like a crowd of invisible people all trying to talk at once.

"You did this," accused Jack, too angry to feel frightened anymore, holding up the skull. "You never drowned, did you? Poll said you could swim. You escaped, and you murdered Blackstrap Morgan. You betrayed the others. And you stole the treasure. It was *you! You* should have been cursed, not him. Not me."

Captain Kelso bared his teeth, looking even more evil than before. "Blackstrap's spawn," he said. "Mayhap that's the truth of it. But, as they say, dead men tell no tales."

He lifted his sword and slashed it through the air.

Suddenly, the whispering rose to a scream. The air became alive. At first, it seemed to be a strange, gusting wind, whipping up the sand, but then Jack saw the shapes of people. Of pirates. He saw a gold earring, a striped shirt, a flying pigtail. Jack ducked, but the pirates ran through and around him as if he wasn't there.

He had a glimpse of a transparent Hellfire Drake, stamping and roaring. And Tortuga Anna, beautiful and furious. He saw the big bearded pirate with the monkey. And there were many more.

He saw Captain Kelso's face turn even paler than before. "Shipmates," he cried. "No, no . . ."

The sight of his former friends, whom he had betrayed, seemed to terrify him. He faltered for a moment. Then he lost his nerve, dropped his sword, turned, and ran. The wind of ghostly pirates swarmed after him.

Captain Kelso ran screaming across the headland. Jack heard his footsteps, heard confused, angry shouting on the wind. Then the footsteps stopped and there was a scream, which went on and on. There was a strange slamming sound, which Jack felt rather than heard. Like a heavy door banging shut in the wind. He felt it through the ground and in the air around him.

Then there was nothing. Just the distant sound of the surf.

Jack found he was trembling all over. He felt shaky and weak. Slowly, he climbed out of the shallow pit, carrying the skull and the hook. Cautiously, he headed in the direction that Captain Kelso had run, right to the tip of the headland. The footprints led all the way to the edge. Jack looked down.

A sheer cliff. It was a long, long way down, and at the bottom waves crashed onto sharp rocks.

Jack found Captain Kelso's sword, where he had dropped it. It was very rusty, and the blade was broken into several pieces. This seemed odd, because it had been shiny and sharp when Jack had last seen it. He thought of taking it with him, but in the end he decided to throw it over the cliff.

Later, Jack didn't remember much about going back down through the jungle, clutching Blackstrap Morgan's skull and the hook. The path wound around, down and down, and he kept expecting to come out at the beach where he had started. He had the strange feeling that things were disappearing behind him, the headland, the waterfall, the jungle. He knew he'd never be back here again. The curse was finished.

Eventually, the path flattened out. Jack noticed that the jungle beside the path had been recently cut back, and he almost tripped over a pile of branches. He heard voices calling him. Suddenly, he felt dizzy. He stumbled—then everything went black.

 CHAPTER 15

When Jack opened his eyes some time later, he was lying down.

Immediately, he saw Poll's face, very concerned, very close, and upside down.

"Poll," he said, weak with relief. He'd never been so happy to see anyone. He looked around. He was in the backyard. In the clearing, near the pool. He was vaguely interested to see that the jungle was still there, even though the curse had ended. Dad would probably have to chop it all down to get rid of it. "What happened?" Jack asked.

Poll gave a cluck. "Pieces of eight, pieces of eight," he squawked.

Jack sat up with a jerk that made his head spin. He remembered what Poll had said, that before the curse he had just been a normal parrot. No conversation.

Jack felt a terrible sadness. It was like losing a friend. Poll was still there, but now he was just a—

Poll gave a sudden screech of laughter. He fell off Jack's head and lay on his back on the mossy ground, laughing and laughing, his claws waving helplessly.

"Your face, shipmate," he gasped. "To see your face. Ha ha ha ha ha!"

Jack sat up. "You, you . . ." He glared down at the helplessly laughing parrot. "You . . ." He couldn't think of anything to say that would be angry enough. He wished he had learned some pirate curses while he had the chance. "It's not that funny," he said lamely.

"Oh, it is, shipmate," gasped Poll.

Mom and Dad rushed into the clearing.

"Jack, oh, Jack!" cried Mom. "Are you all right? We've been looking everywhere for you. What happened? Where were you?" She knelt down on the wet, muddy ground and gave Jack a big hug.

"I'm fine," he said, his voice muffled, hugging her back. Feeling safe.

"Are you sure?" asked Mom, giving him a small shake. "What happened? We've been searching for ages. Don't ever do anything like that again. I was so worried."

"Don't worry, Mom," said Jack. "I don't think I'll be able to, anyway. The curse is over. Finished."

Dad picked up the skull and the hook. "Oh, good," he said, but with just a hint of disappointment in his voice.

That night, Jack sat with Rachel at the edge of the pool, feet in the water, watching the party.

There had been a mountainous bonfire earlier, but now it had died down to a gently sparking mound. Mom had put glass lanterns with candles in them along the path from the back door and around the pool, and they glimmered cheerfully against the dark jungle.

Mom had invited Mrs. Lemon and Mr. Stockton to the party, as a sort of apology for all the trouble. Mrs. Lemon was dancing the hornpipe with Dad, both of them stamping and roaring like Hellfire Drake. Mr. Stockton was keeping time, shouting, "One, Two, One, Two."

Mom and Doctor van Donkel were singing. Earlier, these two had had a fork-throwing competition. They set up a potato on the other side of the pool and flung silverware at it until it looked like a porcupine.

Rachel's parents were reclining in deckchairs, sipping rum and looking happy, although somewhat confused. Doctor Zoob was cheerfully eating his fifth plate of roasted breadfruit and plum duff.

Poll was perched on Jack's head, hopping up and down, singing as loudly as possible, and giving the occasional ear-splitting screech.

It was too loud for conversation, so Jack just listened, watching the sparks from the fire fly upward to join the stars in the night sky.

Shipmates all through storm and squall,
Across the briny sea,
Rant and roar and treasure galore,
A pirate's life for me.

ACKNOWLEDGMENTS

Thank you to Hazel Edwards, the class at Holmesglen TAFE, Lorette, Ben, Linda, and Ruth.